Nicole suddenly froze in place.

"Don't move," she said. "Don't speak."

"Another spider?" Flynn asked, his voice rising a few octaves. "Horribly poisonous multi-legged insect?"

She scanned the Amazon jungle around them, then shook her head. "We're surrounded."

Flynn looked around warily. "I don't see anybody," he said.

Suddenly, a swarm of native tribesmen were on all sides of them. Each carried a spear or a primitive bow or a handful of darts.

"Oh," said Flynn. *"Them."*

Nicole nodded. "Them," she agreed.

WORLDS OF ADVENTURE
Published by ibooks, inc.

Ghostbusters: The Return
by Sholly Fisch

Gauntlet: Dark Legacy
Book 1: Paths of Evil
by Richard C. White

The Transformers Legends
David Cian, Editor

Terminator 2: Hour of the Wolf
by Mark W. Tiedemann

Battlestar Galactica: Destiny
by Richard Hatch
and Brad Linaweaver

Defender: Hyperswarm
by Tim Waggoner

THE ADVENTURES OF
THE LIBRARIAN™

QUEST FOR THE SPEAR

NOVELIZATION BY
CHRISTOPHER TRACY

BASED ON THE TELEPLAY BY
DAVID TITCHER

INTRODUCTION BY
DEAN DEVLIN

ibooks
new york
www.ibooks.net

DISTRIBUTED BY SIMON & SCHUSTER, INC.

An Original Publication of ibooks, inc.

The Librarian ™ and copyright © 2004
ApolloProScreen GmbH & Co. Filmproduktion KG.
All rights reserved.

Based on the teleplay by David Titcher

ibooks, inc.
24 West 25th Street
New York, NY 10010

The ibooks World Wide Web Site Address is:
www.ibooks.net

ISBN 1-4165-0486-9
First ibooks, inc. printing November 2004
10 9 8 7 6 5 4 3 2 1

Edited by Steven A. Roman

Special thanks to Dean Devlin, Kearie Peak,
Paige Hardwick, and Rand Marlis
for their invaluable help.

Cover photograph of Noah Wyle copyright © 2004
ApolloProScreen GmbH & Co. Filmproduktion KG

Cover design by Mat Postawa

Printed in the U.S.A.

*This one's for
Steve Roman, the "good" cop.
May God have mercy on your soul.*

Introduction

By Dean Devlin

What if? That's the magical question that has sparked a million imaginative adventures throughout the centuries: What if? *The Adventures of The Librarian* centers on such a question: What if there was a hidden and secretive library that held all of the mysterious and magical treasures found throughout mankind's history? Such things as The Golden Fleece, Thor's Hammer, The Holy Grail. What if there was a secret organization dedicated to procuring and securing these items, keeping them safe and out of the hands of those who do not wish us well?

That is the basic premise that author David Titcher brought to my company. He had fashioned a whimsical adventure around this Librarian and his quest to return a powerful talisman back to the safety of the Library. Instantly I thought this was a fantastic "what if" story that I'd love to help bring to the screen. Purely by coincidence, it was just at that time that I got a call from one of my agents, who said, "You have to meet with TNT."

So, as we often do in Tinseltown, I was invited to have lunch with Michael Wright, a bigwig at the television network TNT. He expressed a fondness for the films that I've made, and we shared a passion for the same kinds of stories. Michael said he'd like to develop a television movie with the same kind of energy, scale, humor and adventure.

I told him about *The Librarian*. By the flash in his eyes, you could see that he could already envision our heroes slashing their way through the dense Amazon Jungle in search of a magical item that must be returned to the Library. He visualized our heroes climbing the snow-covered mountains of the Himalayan Mountains, or deciphering hieroglyphics in the Great Pyramid of Egypt. He was able to see in his mind's eye the final film, just off the rough pitch of the idea. Immediately he bought the project.

In true collaboration with TNT, we have put together what I think is one of the best pieces of material I've ever been associated with—not only as an outstanding original screenplay, but also as a larger story and mythology that seems to grow each day with a life of its own. I find myself wanting to watch these characters develop and wanting to know more about their adventures. There are extraordinary stories hidden in the Library. We begin with one of my favorites, The Librarian featured in this story, Flynn Carson.

We have been very fortunate to have great actors interpret our story. Kyle MacLachlan, Bob Newhart, Jane Curtin, and Academy Award-winner Olympia Dukakis are internationally famous. Sonya Walger, David Dayan Fisher, and Kelly Hu soon will be.

Foremost in our cast is our brilliant lead actor, Noah Wyle. Noah was a key partner in making the story come to life and developing who Flynn Carson ultimately became. Noah has a nearly encyclopedic memory, especially when it comes to film history. Not only was he well versed in all the genre films we meant to pay tribute to, he educated us to a few as well. He immediately understood the character better than we did. It was so strange watching him become this character as it was so unlike anything he had ever done professionally before.

Known as a dramatic and quite serious actor, I don't think any of us were prepared for his absolute ease with comedic timing, and his incredible ability to transform himself into this character. A character so boldly portrayed, so wonderfully original, that I don't think anyone who watches this film will ever see him the same way again.

The character of Flynn Carson is the ultimate armchair quarterback. In his early thirties, Flynn Carson still finds himself living at home with his mother, still a student at the University. He's not there because he's slow. No, in fact, quite the opposite. Flynn is still there because he can't get enough of it. He's addicted to learning. Every time he gets a degree, he desires another one. He's what's known in academia as "a professional student."

While he knows something about everything, he has virtually no "hands on" experience with anything. On a particularly snowy week, he was once invited to go skiing with some other students. While he didn't travel with them, he joined them, nonetheless, in the only fashion that suits him: he raced to the school's library, looked up every book he could on skiing—the sport, the science behind it, its history, and the names and maps of every ski resort in the world. And memorized them.

So when Flynn Carson finally ventures off into the world to find himself, he discovers there's no substitute for experience. Yet no experience for which he hasn't read, studied or theorized about. In a sense, he's familiar with that which he is unfamiliar. For me, he is a completely unique hero, one told with a great deal of humor, fun and pathos. His super-power is not one of the body, or super-human abilities, it's simply his incredibly well-developed mind.

I love the idea of a story that ultimately reminds us that the greatest adventures we have can only be appreciated through thought, can only be memorialized through literature, documentation and memorization. As our character Judson, the wise head of the Library, tells Flynn Carson before he goes off on his first adventure, "Remember, the most important item is not held in The Library." Then, touching Flynn's temporal lobe, he adds, "Its right up here."

Often I've heard people describe science fiction, adventure, and fantasy stories as "escapist" tales meant to take us away and escape our existence into an enchanting world that doesn't really exist. While I don't dispute that there is a great deal of truth to that sentiment, I'd like to also suggest that sometimes, by taking things out of the specific, and allowing the discussion to take place in the abstract, we can sometimes see things that our prejudices would not allow us to see.

For instance, I remember as a child that *Star Trek* would often take on issues such as racism and the Vietnam War and put it in the abstract reality of the science fiction television show. Suddenly, people I knew who were on opposite sides of the argument could find common ground when dealing with it in this kind of metaphor.

I guess what I'm suggesting is that not only can these kinds of stories expand our imagination, they can also, occasionally, offer us a unique view of that which is right in front of us to give us a new perspective on things. I know it has for me.

Quest for the Spear is the first in a series of *The Librarian* adventures. I think you'll find enough adventure, humor, arcane knowledge, and puzzles to keep your interest. I hope you have as much fun reading this story as we did creating it.

— *Dean Devlin*
September 2004

PROLOGUE

Late 4th Century, A.D.

The Great Library of Alexandria was burning. Flames and ash rose into the air in whirls and pillars. Popping and cracking sounds echoed in the courtyard as the stones of the buildings themselves cracked in the intense heat. It would be said that rioters had started the blaze and no bucket carriers, not even a whole phalanx of them, could stop it.

The Librarian knew better, but some knowledge wasn't meant to be shared.

Most of the treasures and artifacts brought here for safekeeping—the written works of every traveling scholar who'd passed this way, the armor of Odysseus, the sword and shield of Perseus, perfect copies of the so-called Dead Sea Scrolls, the staff of Moses, the burial shroud of the Christ, the language keys that allowed them to read even texts from before the Tower of Babel—would be lost to the flames. These and so many others of the highest achievements of mankind would be gone. Already, the slaves were refusing to go inside and attempt to save anything else.

The Librarian sighed. He was soul tired. It had been the work of his and several others' lifetimes to gather and guard these treasures, this accumulated knowledge of things known and unknown. Now much would be lost.

But he would not be the last Librarian, anymore than he'd been the first. And some of the treasures would restore themselves after the blaze died down.

Some, he reminded himself, like the scrolls containing the text of the Egyptian Book of the Dead, would not. In fact, the fires might well release some forces best left contained.

He turned and watched as the ashes of the Library rose into the sky. It was a grim day for humankind, for knowledge.

At his feet, the unconscious man with a strange tattoo on his hand stirred and groaned. His name was Wosret, and there was a large bruise forming at his temple. He and his followers called themselves the Brotherhood of the Serpent—representing the force that had brought Adam and Eve to the knowledge of both good and evil... though there was little doubt in the Librarian's mind that they represented only evil.

Wosret groaned again, lifted his head, and dropped it once more. He was coming around. Apparently, being hit in the head with a large rock wasn't quite enough to kill him.

The Librarian looked at the two slaves who stood nearby, waiting for his orders. "Bind him," he ordered. "Then drop him in the Nile for the crocodiles." His voice was clipped and weary, but the slaves moved with alacrity. They were frightened, he knew. They had never before heard him order the death of anyone, not even a disobedient slave.

The man had to be killed—of that, there was no doubt. If he weren't, his cult would rise again. They would never stop until the Library itself was destroyed, the artifacts it held in their sole possession. And though this repository was now gone, the Library would be rebuilt, either here or elsewhere, in time.

His slaves lifted the man between them, and began carrying him off. The Librarian watched as they neared the riverbank. They paused to bind him, when he suddenly moved, lashing out at one with his sandaled feet, and the other with his fist. They dropped him and he staggered away, diving into the Nile and swimming downstream as fast as he could.

The slaves ran back to him, looking chagrined. "We must humbly apologize, Lord," they said in unison, dropping to their knees.

"Go after him and see to it that my orders are carried out," the Librarian snapped. "He must not escape." He could not leave the Library now to give chase himself. The artifacts that remained must be protected, and he was the only one left to do it.

"Yes, Lord," they said. They rose and ran after the fleeing man.

The Librarian shook his head in sorrow. They were not likely to catch him. Wosret had proven to be a wily and dangerous opponent, and his escape would mean that the Brotherhood of the Serpent would return; would, perhaps, plague the Library for hundreds of years to come in a war without end. Their name or the faces of their members might change, but their tactics and goals would not. The chasm between the two organizations had grown too deep, a philosophical divide that could not be breached.

The Library had always been about the gathering and protection of knowledge; the Brotherhood of the Serpent was about power.

Death and evil followed in their steps wherever they walked.

The Librarian sighed and turned his attention back to the fires.

CHAPTER ONE

Flynn Carson held up the small, hooded lantern, and studied the complex series of hieroglyphics over the shoulder of a crouching student named Burroughs. He was a man of medium height and build, with dark eyes and a rather unruly mop of brown hair that had a tendency to stick up in cowlicks at the slightest provocation. The light flickered, and the student's mouth pursed in concentration, trying to decipher the ancient language.

"I can't find this anywhere," he muttered.

"Of course you can't," Flynn said, shaking his head in dismay. The knowledge needed here was rudimentary, and the student should have known it. "That's because you're focusing on the Fourth Dynasty," he hinted. "There's more to the language than that."

Burroughs stood and stretched. "It's a given that you can do better, I suppose," he said.

Flynn shrugged. He could've done better when he was twenty, let alone now. He handed the lantern to the student and carefully traced the hieroglyphs. "See here? These are from the Third Dynasty, and are regional variants. Probably inscribed by slaves with a slightly different dialect."

Several other students crowded around, and Flynn thought of removing his safari jacket. It had been cool enough earlier in the day, but standing in the press of all these bodies made the close air of the Great Pyramid sweltering. He ignored his discomfort, wiped a bead of sweat from his forehead and pointed. "See this set here?" he asked. "It says, '…and down Through these Stones we can Summon Down the Powers of the Gods—' "

"Slow down, man," one of the students said, scribbling furiously in a small notebook. "I can't write that fast."

Flynn ran a hand along the carefully carved stones, feeling the indentations of the hieroglyphics, the pockmarks in the stones themselves. There was nothing he loved more than this feeling of being connected to something so… intensely ancient and wonderful. The Egyptian culture was one of many he knew, but there was something special about their particular culture and history. Perhaps it was that so little is truly known about them, he thought. He turned and took the lantern back from Burroughs, adjusting the shutter so that the light would be directed toward the inner sanctum of the pyramid.

"A square on every single level," he said. "And no more than a 0.01% error on any of the walls." He pointed out an angle where two walls met. "Look at those support stones along the edge. If any of those were even an inch out of alignment, the entire Great Pyramid would come crashing down around us." Pure wonder lit his face. "How did they do it? How did these… primitive people unlock the universal majesty and mysteries of trigonometry and calculus? Their engineering skills were centuries before their time…"

Flynn handed the lantern back to Burroughs. "Truly amazing," he said, then turned to make his way outside. He wanted to look at the exterior of the structure again.

Exiting the Great Pyramid, he gazed at the beauty of the sand dunes and was struck by their unwavering sameness—yet he knew that a truly observant person could see hundreds and even thousands of distinct patterns in the sand. Nearby, another large group of students grunted and strained on a huge pulley system as they hoisted a gigantic stone high above their heads.

Talking to himself, Flynn paced in front of the historic structure. "For *four thousand years,* until just one hundred years ago, this was the tallest structure on Earth! The Egyptians reached within and even past themselves and grabbed hold of the divine, summoned the Muses, and forged what is indeed the greatest of the original Seven Wonders of the World!"

Standing at the base of the Great Pyramid, he felt himself almost lift free of the ground; to be here, at the base of one of man's greatest achievements, filled him with a sense of awe that he would be hard-pressed to describe. He closed his eyes and could almost feel the desert wind blowing through his already mussed brown hair.

A sudden, squeaking sound startled him out of his reverie. A janitor with a mop bucket touched his shoulder. " 'Scuse me, but somebody spilled a mochaccino?"

Painfully returning to the real world, Flynn nodded. "Oh, yeah," he said. "Right over there." He pointed to a spot on the floor where the model hadn't been completed yet.

"Thanks," the janitor said. He moved toward the spill with all the enthusiasm of a man walking toward the electric chair.

Returning his attention to the Great Pyramid, Flynn tried to recapture the lost moment, but it was gone. *This* Great Pyramid was a scale model, almost eighty feet high, and as exacting of a duplicate of the real thing as the Advanced Egyptology class he was in could make it. The rolling sand dunes were nothing more than well-painted dioramas. The stone the students were trying to hoist up to the top was the Pyramid's capstone, which was, in reality, missing from the real Great Pyramid, but a necessary part of the recreation.

One of the grad students working the hoist, Jack, suddenly yelled out to him. "Hey, Flynn! You want to stop freakin' posing there and join the rest of us?"

Flynn ran to grab the end of the rope, and helped swing the massive capstone into place. It landed atop the Pyramid with a resounding thud. The final piece of the exterior itself. The students, including Flynn, broke into spontaneous applause. It was a moment worth celebrating. They'd been working on this recreation for several long months.

Professor Harris stepped forward. He sported a blonde bowl-cut hairstyle that was going gray at the temples and swept across his forehead. He had a slight build that perfectly suited his wire-rimmed glasses, but possessed an intense energy that most of his students admired. "I want to thank you all for a great semester," he said. "Because of you, the Pyramid Project is off to a wonderful start. And despite what the naysayers would have had us believe, we will show, for the first time, a perfect 1/20th scale model, using *real* Pyramid stones, of exactly what the Great Pyramid looked like when it was first built!" He paused dramatically for a second, then added, "Complete with its missing capstone!"

The students applauded again, excited to be a part of this achievement.

"According to legend," Professor Harris continued, "the capstone focused incredible energies within the Pyramid itself. Once the model is complete, we're going to measure the electromagnetic fields within the structure to try and confirm this. As far as myself and the University is concerned, this is the most exciting event in Egyptology since Howard Carter opened the tomb of King Tut."

As the students' applause washed over the room again, Flynn thought about what a moment *that* would have been, seeing the tomb of the great King Tut opened. So many discoveries found, so much knowledge to be touched and perused.

"All right," Professor Harris said, a smile lighting his pale face. "Enough self-congratulations. Let's get back to work."

As the students returned to their tasks, Flynn worked his way over to his instructor. "Professor Harris?" he said. "About my role here. I was thinking I could be more useful in managing the translation—"

"Flynn, you won't be continuing on with the Pyramid Project," Harris said.

Flynn stopped walking, stunned, before shaking his head and running to catch up. "But, I'm your best student—"

"That's exactly the problem," Harris said. "You *are* my best student. You're *everyone's* best student. You've never been *anything* but the best student." He shook his head. "I'd be doing you, and the other students here who have something to learn, a disservice to let you continue."

"That's… that's unfair," Flynn said. "And confusing. Confusingly unfair. Unfairly con—"

"For God's sake, Flynn," Harris said, interrupting him. "You already have, what? Four degrees in Egyptology? Do you really need a fifth?"

"I'm weak on the Second Dynasty!" he protested. "And relatively useless on the Sixth!"

"How many degrees do you have in total?"

"Not all that many," Flynn said.

"Uh-huh," Harris said. "I've checked your transcripts. You have twelve Bachelor degrees, six Masters, and four PhD's. Twenty-two total. That's got to be some kind of record."

"Alexander Fuller," he said.

"Excuse me?"

"In the 19th century, Alexander Fuller got twenty-seven degrees," Flynn explained. "He died in the middle of writing his thesis for his twenty-eighth."

Harris stared at him for a long moment, then said, "That is *not* a good way to die. I'd hate to see you go that way. Certainly not until you've actually done some *real* living!"

"Professor Harris," Flynn began, feeling a strange sense of desperation in the pit of his stomach, "school is what I know. It's where I belong and... and where I feel like myself. The more I learn, the more I realize how much I don't know. How much there is to learn. There's so much knowledge yet to be discovered."

"Take a look over there," the professor said, pointing to the working students. "You've been in this class for three whole months now. Do you even know any of their names?"

Flynn studied the other members of the class. Most of them were grad students finishing up their PhD work in either Ancient History or Egyptology, who would go on to field work or teaching positions of one kind or another. He wasn't close to any of them; he had little in common with most people, and students without an advanced degree or two in particular.

"Of course I do," he said. "Sort of. Well, I don't know their real names because we all have nicknames."

A student passed by, carrying a load of hand trowels in his arms. "Hey," Flynn said, patting him on the back, "how's it going, Sweater Guy?"

The student paused long enough to mutter, "Freak," before continuing toward his destination.

"Right back at ya," Flynn said, trying to sound hearty and failing miserably.

Harris laid a hand on his shoulder. "You're a professional student, Flynn. You're avoiding life—and *that* is a serious problem that I will no longer enable."

"What are you doing to me here, Professor?"

"Flynn, have you ever even been out of the city?" When he didn't reply, Harris added, "When was the last time you went out dancing with a girl, or went to a ball game?"

"I have a very full life, Professor," Flynn said.

"You need to find a job," Harris said. "Get some actual life experience. Knowledge without wisdom is meaningless. Instead of finding discoveries here, go out and find them in the real world. I've already spoken with the administration and they're in total agreement with me. I've signed off on your degree here. You're done. Congratulations."

"But it's the middle of the semester!" Flynn objected.

"Yes, it is."

"It'll be six months before I can sign up for another program."

"Exactly," Harris said. "Six months of living in the real world, Flynn."

"Don't do this to me, Professor Harris," he pleaded. "All I want to do is learn."

"Not every classroom is in a school," Harris shot back. "We should never stop learning—it's only *where* we learn that changes. And it's past time you started doing it in the big, bad real world. Sink or swim, Flynn—those are your choices."

Prepared to continue his objections, Flynn stopped short when he saw the professor's upraised hand. "We're done here," Harris said. "Good luck." Then he walked away.

Now what the hell do I do? Flynn thought as he slowly walked toward the exhibit exit. *A job? What kind of job could I get? How much call could there be for someone with my background?*

Nearby, he noted a group of students at a table, trying to reassemble hundreds of shattered tile fragments.

He stopped and watched them struggle with the pieces. It was really an elementary puzzle. Finally, unable to take it any longer, he stepped forward. "Here," he said. "It goes like this."

With incredible speed and precision, he began putting the pieces in place. His hands just *knew* where everything belonged. In a few quick moments, the pictograph was completely reassembled. "There," Flynn said, stepping back, feeling satisfied.

When he looked up, he saw a gamut of emotions on the faces of the students—shock, awe, even jealousy. All of them were staring.

"Well… er… that's one way to do it anyway," he said, feeling more awkward than before. *Maybe I am a freak,* he thought.

He offered the students a little wave and continued on his way out of the building. Lost in thought, he didn't notice the man watching him from the balcony overlooking the main floor. A bit stocky and balding, well-dressed, and with a round face showing the lines of a person who'd done some real living, the man made a note in a huge journal.

Stepping outside, Flynn stopped only once— to look back at the ivory towers he had called home for so long. The last step, the one that took him off campus, was harder than he'd ever imagined it would be.

Not that taking such a step had even occurred to him before this day.

He was leaving behind the safe, secure place that had protected and nurtured him for many years. The problem was that he didn't know what he was leaving it for, or where he would end up without it.

Flynn opened the front door. It was a modest home, not particularly fancy but well-appointed and comfortable. It wasn't a home with furniture people didn't sit on or kitchen tables that were always spotless, but it had always felt like a haven, even after his father had died. He had lived here most of his life, yet coming home today was different somehow. Even the sanctuary of his room, filled with his extensive collection of books, would provide little comfort.

Knowing what to expect, but still feeling the sense of dread that only comes when one lives with a parent, he called out, "Mom, I'm home," and kicked the door shut behind him. His arms were loaded down with all his textbooks—books that he wouldn't be using.

"Hi, honey," his mother, Margie, said. "I see my brilliant boy has returned from a long day of getting even more brilliant."

She was a pretty, if slightly vain, woman in her middle fifties. She kept her hair dyed a golden shade of blond, and dressed in a casual style befitting a younger woman. Today she wore an orange-colored tank top with a tan jacket over it, and matching slacks. A necklace and turquoise earrings completed her ensemble, which had a vaguely southwestern flair to it.

She made tweaking Flynn a daily priority. Judging by her expression, today would be no different.

"Mom, please," he said. "Not today."

He headed for his room, but his mom was close on his heels. Opening the door, Flynn nudged aside a towering stack of books to make room on the floor for his latest batch.

Tripping over one of the many volumes scattered across his floor, Margie said, "Books! Books! Books! How do you even sleep in here?"

"Soundly," he said, bending down and picking up several titles. He held them tightly to his chest, valued treasures and friends for his entire life. Reading and studying had always brought him a great sense of satisfaction—he'd traveled the world, explored distant planets, discussed philosophy and psychology and every other 'ology' with the greatest minds of human history.

As a child, reading had been an escape that had grown into a passion for learning and scholarship that had never deserted him, never left him. People may die, civilizations falter, but their knowledge lived on for those willing to study.

He held up the books he'd retrieved from the floor. "Voltaire, Aristotle, Jung. These books are slices of the ultimate truth from the greatest thinkers who ever lived." He placed the books on an overflowing shelf. "They speak to me, Mom."

Margie's face softened slightly, and she took his arm. "They speak to you."

"Yes, like nothing or no one else ever has."

"Do they…" Margie's voice trailed off, then she said. "Do they tell you to do bad things?"

She was incorrigible. He should have seen it coming. "I'm going out," he said.

"Do they tell you to set fires, Flynn?" she asked, laughing, continuing to needle him. "Don't listen to the books if they tell you to set fires or hurt small animals—"

"I'll be at the bookstore, Mom," Flynn said, desperate to escape. The day had been long enough already without this torture. Bad enough having to leave the university and get a job.

Just as he reached the front hall, the door-bell rang.

"Oh, good," Margie said, grabbing his arm once more. "She's here."

"Who?" he asked, fearing the answer.

"She's a nice girl," his mother said. "You'll like her. You'll say hello." She began dragging him toward the front door, while simultaneously trying to straighten his unruly hair. "One thing," she added. "Don't do what you always do."

Flynn felt a protest building, but before he could voice it, Margie opened the door. An attractive woman with brunette hair, about twenty-eight years old, was just about to ring the bell again.

"Debra, Flynn. Flynn, Debra. You two look great together," Margie said.

"Hello, Flynn," Debra said. "It's nice to meet you."

Flynn sighed. There was no point in trying to escape now. His mother would have a genuine fit. It would be better to just go through with the charade to keep the peace. "Hi," he said.

"I'll leave you kids alone," Margie said. She headed toward the kitchen.

"Would you like to come in and sit down?" Flynn asked, moving aside so Debra could enter and gesturing in the direction of the living room.

Once they were seated on the sofa, a long moment of silence ensued. Flynn wasn't sure what to say, and Debra didn't seem too certain either.

Finally, she said, "This is weird, I know."

"How'd my mom…?"

"Friends with *my* mom. They're so obsessed with us getting into relationships, you know?"

Feeling a sudden sense of camaraderie, Flynn said, "Yes! That's it exactly!"

"You'd think we were sitting around the house, locked in our rooms and reading textbooks for fun and pleasure," Debra added.

His feeling of having found a kindred spirit evaporated rapidly. "Umm… yeah," Flynn said. Trying to change the subject, he asked, "So… Debra, what do you do?"

"I'm a social worker," she said.

"That's great," he said. "Do you work with children or the elderly or…"

"Killers, mainly," she said. "Mostly convicted felons."

Flynn felt his jaw creak open and snapped it shut before she could note his reaction.

"What do you do, Flynn?"

"I'm at the university," he said.

"Really?" Debra asked, interest sparking in her eyes. "A professor?"

"No—"

"Administration, then," Debra said, charging ahead full speed. She was obviously used to having to talk over the killers in her life. "I know Dean Gray. He's a wonderful man."

"No, no!" Flynn said, attempting to head her off at the pass. "I'm a student."

"A student?" she asked, still running in a higher gear than Flynn was comfortable with.

"Yep," he said.

"You went back to school!" she said. "That's wonderful."

"I... ah... technically, I never really left," he said. Noting her look of disbelief, he added,

"Technically."

Debra processed this information for a long moment, then said, "You've been a college student your entire adult life."

Feeling more than a little defensive after the day he'd just had, Flynn said, "So I enjoy learning. So what? Is that a crime?"

"Nooo..." Debra said.

"So maybe I've spent—" he paused "—most to all of my life in school. Maybe I *have* missed out on some extra-curricular activities. That doesn't make me a freak."

"Of course it doesn't," Debra said in the same tone that he imagined she used on psychotic killers. "I understand." She patted him on the knee.

"You do?" Flynn asked, hating the desperate sound in his voice.

"Sure. You like to learn."

"Yes," he said.

"And you're in your thirties and you're still in school."

"That's right," he said. To hell with it, he thought. I've achieved a lot!

"And you live with your mother and you're all right with all of this?"

"Yes. No. Wait a minute—" Flynn said.

Debra watched him, her expression pleasant, obviously prepared to wait for him to string it all together.

It stung to admit that not only was she right, but maybe Professor Harris had a point, too. Being a professional student did have certain limitations, but until now he'd never given them much thought.

"I have *really* got to change my life, don't I?" he asked.

"I would," she suggested.

From the kitchen, Margie called out, "Is anybody hungry?" She followed the sound of her own voice into the living room, bearing a tray of finger sandwiches.

Debra stood up. "I wish I could stay, Mrs. Carson, but I really have to get back to work.

My job is a killer." She laughed at her own joke, and Flynn forced a weak chuckle.

"You're going?" Margie said. "So soon?"

Debra moved toward the front door. "It was nice meeting you, Flynn," she said. "Good luck to you. Change is never easy, but I hope things turn out all right for you."

He nodded. "Thanks. I hope so, too."

Debra smiled, waved, and went out. Flynn and his mother shared a sigh, though for entirely different reasons.

"Mom, don't do that anymore, okay?" he asked.

"I just want my boy to find love!" Margie said. "Is that such a crime?"

"I will, mom. One day. When it's right."

His mom stepped forward and grasped him by the arms. For a moment, he feared she was about to start needling him again, then she smiled. "Flynn," she said, "your head is so clogged with facts that you don't know what's really important. The things that make life worth living can't be *thought* up here—" she pointed to his head "—they must be felt *here*." She pointed to his heart. "Maybe, just maybe, you don't know as much as you think you do." Flynn didn't reply as Margie picked up the sandwich tray and left the room.

CHAPTER TWO

The "Help Wanted" section of *The New York Times* proved to be a daunting minefield of jobs that had little to do with Flynn's educational background, mixed with jobs that had little to do with anything he was willing to consider doing. He'd circled a few lame possibilities, but they were more akin to betting on a three-legged long shot in the Kentucky Derby than any job he really wanted.

In short, looking for a real job was a frustrating pain in the ass.

Without appearing from behind his newspaper, Flynn noticed Margie open the door and deposit a small stack of mail on one of his over-loaded bookshelves. She shut the door quietly, and he tossed the paper down in disgust. He'd never had a real job in his life, and getting one now was going to be—at best—a six-month ordeal until he could get signed up at the university again. Why should he even bother?

He pulled a book from the shelf, *The Illustrated Glossary to Plant Identification in the Americas,* glanced at it and dropped it on the floor. He'd read it several times and, though it was quite good, it no longer held any magic for him. His eye caught the title of another book— *A Field Guide to Venomous Insects and Spiders—* and he pulled it down as well. Opening it, he began reading, then just as suddenly stood up and threw it as hard as he could against the door.

"Damn it!" he yelled. What was the point in re-reading material he'd memorized long ago?

He flung himself down on the floor, his back slamming into a bookcase, which tipped precariously on impact. Books rained down off the overfilled shelves, and he covered his head with his arms. "Woah!" he said, trying to avoid being hit with one of the volumes. When the rain of literature stopped, Flynn looked at the books scattered across the floor.

The room was filled to overflowing with books, the shelves ready to topple. There were books on his bed, his nightstand, *under* the bed, and everywhere else in the room. And...

Flynn sighed. They held absolutely nothing of true interest for him. The magic was gone, and whatever he needed to do with his life would not be found within those pages.

Slowly, like feathers borne on an errant breeze, the mail that Margie had brought in earlier floated down from the shelf. One of the envelopes, plain white with gold piping, caught Flynn's eye, and he picked it up. It was addressed to him in a formal, almost antique-looking script. He opened the envelope and removed a completely blank sheet of white paper.

"Now that's a waste of—" he almost added the word "paper" to his statement, but was interrupted by a beautiful, enchanting melody... that was coming *from* the paper. The music was light and inviting, like he imagined the folk of the Sidhe might play beneath a full moon in long-ago Ireland. "How'd you do that?" Flynn asked, studying the sheet for clues.

Just as suddenly as the music had begun, the white paper changed color, becoming an inviting shade of gold, the color of wheat nearing harvest. Words began appearing on the page in a neat calligraphy—as though an invisible hand were writing them—and Flynn felt himself staring in open-mouthed amazement at this phenomenon.

He read the words aloud as they appeared: "You have been selected to interview for a prestigious position with the New York Metropolitan Public Library." Flynn shook his head. "I'll be damned," he muttered, watching as a time and place was given for the interview.

"Hey, Mom!" he called out, intrigued by the novelty of the invitation. "You won't believe it, but I've got a job interview!"

"For what?" she yelled, unbelieving, as she raced into the room.

Flynn studied the sheet again. "Er... ummm... I don't know exactly. A librarian?"

The New York Metropolitan Library was a sprawling complex of white marble and Ionic columns. The location had been spelled out very clearly in the invitation—the office directly at the top of the grand staircase in the main building. As Flynn opened the front doors, he was surprised to see a long line of people winding up the stairs. Many of them were holding resumés and had obviously received the same invitation that he had.

Flynn stood at the back of the line, holding his résumé and wondering what the job was really about, when a woman hurried down the steps. The tears running down her face and the frantic way she clutched at her résumé made it obvious that her interview had not gone well.

From within the office at the top of the steps, a harsh female voice yelled, "Next!"

The line continued to move forward, and when Flynn was halfway up the stairs, yet another applicant hurried down the steps. This time it was an older man, and his red-faced, angry demeanor showed that he hadn't done well, either.

"Next!" the woman from the office yelled.

Flynn looked down at his résumé, which was really nothing more than an extensive *curriculum vitae,* and winced. He had no practical experience whatsoever—what kind of chance did he really have? Of his twelve Bachelor degrees, none of them were in Library Science, though he did have English Literature, Psychology, Sociology, Biology, Political Science, History, Anthropology, Chemistry, Mathematics, Physics, Spanish, Russian, German, French, and American Indian Studies. His Masters work included a Juris Doctorate in Law, Archeology, Egyptology, and three degrees in ancient cultures and languages. All his PhD work had been in Egyptology, with the exception of one he'd gotten almost by accident in Botanical Studies.

He sighed. It was the résumé of the consummate bookworm, a nerd without a home.

The line continued to move upward, with each interviewee returning down the steps wearing looks ranging from sadness and anger to chagrin and disappointment. The invisible woman's voice continued to yell, "Next!" as each candidate for the "prestigious position" was rejected.

Flynn began to wonder if this was a job he really wanted, let alone wanted to interview for—the woman conducting the screenings was obviously a harridan. Did most job interviews end with people crying?

He'd reached the front of the line when the woman called out, "Next!" at the same time as he'd decided to leave. Flynn turned to go, but stopped short when the woman said, "Where do you think *you're* going?"

Realizing she meant him, he turned around reluctantly.

"Yes, you!" the woman called out. "Get in here!"

The open door of the office beckoned and Flynn stepped inside to find a huge room that was empty except for a large, hand-carved mahogany desk. To one side, a pale white desk lamp provided illumination. Seated behind it was the woman who owned the harsh voice—a shorter woman with a rounded face and rather severe reddish hair cut short at her jawline. Her clothes were conservative, too; a black suit with a white top beneath it. Her use of cosmetics was minimal and served only to highlight her angry eyes. All in all, her look matched the pinched expression on her face, the one that made her look as though she'd swallowed a lemon, and Flynn wondered if her first career wasn't with the Internal Revenue Service, perhaps in the "CONGRATS, YOU'RE OFFICIALLY SCREWED" Division.

The room was stuffy, like those in most libraries, and the lighting poor. Flynn had spent more time in one library or another than anyone else he knew, so at least the environment was comfortable. He handed her his résumé—which was slightly rumpled from his folding it back and forth while he waited in line—and sat down in the chair across from her.

"What makes you think you could be The Librarian?" she snapped.

Knowing he was doomed, Flynn said, "I've read a lot of books?" *A librarian,* he thought. *All this for a job as a librarian?*

She put his résumé down on her desk. "Don't try to be funny. I don't do funny."

"Sorry."

Flynn stared at the woman in silence, waiting for her to berate him or yell her hallmark "Next!"

or something. Finally, remembering Professor Harris' advice that he get some *real* experience, he said, "Look, I really need this job."

"Then answer my question. What makes you think you could be *The* Librarian?"

"I know the Dewey Decimal, Library of Congress system, research paper orthodoxy, web searching. I could set up an RSS feed—"

"Everybody knows how to do that. They're librarians." She shook her head. "What makes you think you're *The* Librarian?"

Trying to come up with a suitable answer, Flynn fumbled for words. "I know… other stuff, too."

"Mister—" the woman looked down at his résumé "—Flynn Carson. Stop wasting my time. Tell me something you know that nobody else who walked in here could tell me."

Flynn studied her briefly. He'd done this any number of times in the past, usually when he was trying to get a date. It didn't often work. "Okay," he said. "I'll tell you four things." He held up his fingers, ticking them off as he spoke. "One, you're coming down with mononucleosis. Two, your marriage broke up two months ago.

Three, you broke your nose when you were four. And four, you live with three cats."

The woman's mouth dropped open in shock, and for a long moment Flynn was afraid she'd stopped breathing. He'd had that happen once when he told a prospective date that she exhibited all the signs of someone with an imminent and undetected heart condition. He'd revived her with CPR.

"Is that what you meant?" he asked, hoping he wasn't facing the same situation or worse.

The woman continued to stare blankly. Had she had a stroke?

"Look, it wasn't that difficult." He pointed to her face. "Swollen parajugular lymph nodes and slightly distended eyelids. Clearly mono. You should probably see your doctor about that." His gaze moved to her ring finger. "The indentation on a ring finger takes about three months to completely fade. Yours is two-thirds gone." He gestured back toward her face. "The plastic surgeon gave you a terminus paralateral scar, which is only given to children under six. And…" He paused, squinting at her clothing. "I can see three distinct types of cat hair: a white Himalayan, a Tortoiseshell, and an orange-striped Tabby."

Trying to recover, she said, "I didn't break my nose until I was five."

Flynn nodded, and said, "Ah, well then." He stood to leave, assuming he had failed.

"WHAT'S MORE IMPORTANT THAN KNOWLEDGE?" a male voice boomed across the room.

Flynn turned to find the speaker, but didn't see him. "Where'd that come from?" he asked the woman.

"Just answer the question," she said.

Flynn considered it for a moment, then remembered what his mother had said to him the day before. While he wasn't certain that he agreed with her—his whole life had been about acquiring knowledge—she was wiser than he and could well have a point.

"Uh... uh, the things that make life worth living can't be thought here—" he pointed to his head "—they must be felt... here." And he pointed to his heart.

The room was silent, and the expression of the woman sitting at the desk was blank. Suddenly, she stood and walked to the door, throwing it open. Her short heels clicked on the tiled floor.

From where he stood, Flynn heard her say, "The interviews are over. All of you go home."

Flynn began walking toward the exit when she stopped him. "Not you," she said. "My name is Charlene, and I'm the one who makes and enforces the rules. You've got a six-month trial period. You don't screw up, then you will officially be *The* Librarian. Until then, if you're a minute late, I dock your pay. Break anything, I dock your pay. Make me cranky, I dock your pay. Got it?"

Without giving voice to the thought that the "make me cranky" part was obviously unfair, Flynn asked, "Can I at least know *why* you're hiring me? Just so I know what to do the next time I apply for a job."

A man entered the room from somewhere, though Flynn didn't see or hear a door open. He was stocky and balding, but moved with a confident stride. His hands and face showed the lines of a lifetime of work and caring. And he was smiling.

"There isn't going to be a next time, Mr. Carson," he said. His voice had a rough, pleasant undercurrent to it. "You're about to begin a wondrous adventure—and you will never be the same again."

He motioned for Flynn to follow him, and a bookcase opened, revealing a hidden passage. "Let me show you where you'll be working."

The hallway behind the bookcase was empty, though elegant in its appointments. Wood paneling and framed paintings, landscapes mixed with the occasional portrait, and colorful vases in small alcoves made the walk a pleasant one. A faint echo of their footsteps followed them down the passageway. Open doorways led off into the rest of the library, and Flynn found himself glancing into each as they passed. Like most libraries, the rooms he saw were filled with row upon row of shelved books. Which didn't explain much.

What in the world, he wondered, *was the Librarian, instead of a librarian?*

The man continued down the hall, not even glancing into the open doors they passed. "Umm…

excuse me," Flynn said. "I don't even know your name."

"Judson," the man said, pulling up short. "Ah, here we are."

Two large men dressed in dark blue security uniforms appeared out of the shadows. They were both armed with handguns, a nightstick, and some kind of spray canister. Both of them looked capable of handling any intruder.

"I'll admit I've never worked in a library before," Flynn said. "Or anywhere else for that matter, I suppose. But I *have* been in lots of libraries. Isn't this kind of a lot of security to guard a bunch of books?"

Judson smiled. "This is one of the most impenetrable places on Earth, Mr. Carson. Soon enough, you'll understand why."

The two guards escorted them to a large bookcase at the end of the hall. Judson smiled again at Flynn, who felt more than a little bewildered.

"'If we shadows have offended, think but this and all is mended'—" he said.

"'That you have but slumbered here, whilst these visions did appear,'" Flynn immediately replied. "One of my Bachelor degrees is in English Literature."

"I know," Judson said, then gestured toward the bookcase.

Flynn scanned the shelves, then said, "Shakespeare's *A Midsummer Night's Dream,* right?" He pulled the title from the shelf, and suddenly the entire bookcase slid away. Behind it, in a small room, a closed elevator door appeared. The two guards stepped forward and in lockstep each one inserted a key into slots on either side of the elevator doors. They counted off to three and turned them simultaneously.

Somewhat bemused, Flynn said, "Isn't that what the Army does with nuclear missiles?"

Judson chuckled. "Where do you think the Army got the idea?" He stepped into the elevator.

Flynn followed, and the doors closed behind them.

A quick ride down—at least several stories, by Flynn's estimation—and the doors opened once more to reveal yet another security measure: a vault-style room with frosted glass doors. Judson stepped across the room, his footfalls silent, and pushed lightly on a blank patch of wall to reveal a hidden alarm panel.

He tapped out a sequence on the numbered and lettered keys of the touchpad, each one lighting as he pressed it. A green light flickered once on the panel and within the frosted glass of the doors themselves.

"Only a handful of people have ever seen what you are about to see," Judson said.

He gestured for Flynn to step forward, and they waited as the doors slowly swung open on pneumatic hinges. On the other side, a wall of darkness appeared, then overhead lights began to turn on in rows. As each one lit, the sheer size of the room began to take form. It was immense, a space the size of an airplane hanger, perhaps larger.

"How could…" Flynn began. "What the…" he tried again.

Judson laughed. "All will be made clear, Flynn," he said. "Come on."

A short flight of steps led down into the room, which had been hewn from solid rock. The walls arched high overhead in natural stone, but what truly amazed were the contents of the room itself. Flynn turned his head this way and that to try and take it all in. As far as he could see, there were row upon row of treasures and wonders. In the center of the room, two rows of lighted display cases with tables for study between them ran all the way back to the end of the room. Books, scrolls and various manuscripts were shelved along either wall, also running the length of the room.

The nearest display caught his gaze, and Flynn ran forward to look at it. Muttering to himself, he said, "Two and a half cubits in length. Setin wood. Gold overlay." He turned to Judson. "This is a perfect replica of the lost Ark of the Covenant."

"It's not a replica," Judson said.

Flynn reached out a hand to touch the Ark, and Judson snatched his wrist, pulling him away. "If you touch it, you'll be electrocuted," he said. "Or, as they used to say, 'smote down.' Just like the 40,000 Canaanites who battled the Israelites."

Flynn looked around. "Am I on TV? Is this one of those hidden camera kind of things?"

"Trust me, Flynn," Judson said. "This is your destiny."

Together, they walked from one wonder to another. Each of them was marked with a placard in simple script. In one display, a golden coat of wool labeled THE GOLDEN FLEECE. At another nearby, a familiar painting had a placard that read THE MONA LISA.

Flynn shook his head. "Okay. No. Not real. This is not real."

"It is," Judson insisted. "You are now the guardian of these great treasures."

Swallowing, Flynn pointed at the painting. "So what's hanging in the Louvre?"

"You think we'd leave the real one in a public museum?"

Shaking his head, Flynn allowed himself to be led further into the room.

"We loved your paper on Da Vinci's relationship with the model," Judson said.

"I did that in fourth grade!" Flynn said. "How could you possibly know about it?"

"As you might imagine, we're quite careful about who we allow to be The Librarian."

They stopped at another display. An ornate metallic box, hinged, with figures carved along the top, was situated on a cushion. Flynn opened the box and was momentarily mesmerized by a swirling glow of light from within. A sudden chill ran up his spine as dark, winged forms appeared within the light and surged toward the opening.

Judson slammed the lid shut. "Used to belong to a girl named Pandora," he said. "She opened it and evil ruled the planet for a thousand years. Probably best not to repeat her mistake."

Flynn backed away, disbelieving. "This is all impossible," he said. "And, might I add, *very* impossible."

Judson held out his hand. "Cell phone," he said.

Flynn shrugged. He reached into his jacket pocket, then pulled out his cell phone and put it in Judson's hand.

"You talk in there and somebody far away can hear you. No wires. Impossible. This would've been in the Library even fifty years ago. You would've been burned at the stake for it three hundred years ago." Judson handed back the phone, then gestured at the displays. "Right now some of these items may violate the known laws of science, but that's just because our tiny brains haven't figured out the law to explain them."

Flynn turned to another shelf and noted a futuristic-looking weapon. The placard read…

"Tesla's Death Ray?" he said. "There were legends he actually built it, but—"

"You'll soon discover that many of the so-called 'legends' are true. In fact, we encourage those beliefs because it makes our job easier."

Flynn picked up the gun.

"Tesla built and fired it, just once. In 1908. Took out half of Siberia."

"Tunguska!" Flynn said. "That's why no meteor crater was found." He carefully set the gun back on the shelf.

Judson pointed to another shelf, filled with one doomsday device after another. "Each one of those devices could destroy the world. If The Librarian at the time hadn't confiscated them, the world *would've* been destroyed in 1321, 1599, 1872 and 1985. There are those who would kill for the treasures we have in here. And we can't allow them to fall into the wrong hands."

"What… what is this place?" Flynn whispered.

"We call it the Library of Sciences Unknown," Judson said. "Makes sense, doesn't it?"

Flynn stopped at a large stone with a sword stuck in it. "This can't actually be *the* Excalibur!"

"Only the worthy can release it from the stone," Judson said. "Try it."

Thinking, Flynn raised his hand toward the hilt of the sword, then stopped and grinned.

"Yeah. Not worthy. Trust me."

"And how do you know if you don't even try?"

Flynn shook his head and moved on. Behind him, he heard Judson sigh and follow. "I'm not even sure why you chose me."

"We scour the education system," he said. "Public and private, of a few hundred countries. We review essays, doctorate theses—we even read those accursed online blogs."

"So there *is* a system," Flynn said.

"There's a system for finding the candidates," Judson replied. "As for choosing The Librarian, well… that has an odd way of working itself out. Destiny, perhaps." Noting Flynn's look of doubt, he added, "All your life you've been studying. Now you know why."

On a cushion, Flynn saw an old apple with two distinct bites taken out of it. He felt himself break into a huge smile. "Is this what I think it is?" he asked, the excitement in his voice uncontainable.

"Oh, yes," Judson said.

"*The* Apple from the Garden of Eden?"

Judson took the apple from Flynn's hand... and then took another bite out of it!

"Wha—" Flynn managed, before Judson's grin stopped him.

"Oh, no," he said. "That's *my* apple. I lost it in here a few days ago."

Satisfied, Flynn said, "I can't wait to tell my mom about all of this. She'll freak—"

Before the rest of the words could leave his mouth, the jeweled sword of Excalibur was at his throat. The keen edge dug gently at the skin of his neck.

Judson calmly took another bite of his apple. "You're now part of a very special community, Flynn. The secrets of the Library have been kept for thousands of years."

"Sword. Floating. Neck. Help," Flynn choked out, hoping he wouldn't make the sword angry.

"You can't tell anybody about any of this," Judson continued. "Only the Librarians know that this place even exists." He leaned toward the sword and said, "Give Flynn some time. You'll like him."

The sword floated backward, paused as though considering a quick impalement, then turned and flew away, placing itself back within the stone.

CHAPTER THREE

The casket was constructed of mahogany, detailed with scrollwork and mother-of-pearl inlay. If it hadn't been made specifically for holding a dead body, it would have worked beautifully as coffee table. Flynn glanced around, confirming that Judson had left him to his own devices. The placard in front of the coffin read: NOSFERATU, but... He had to know.

He slowly eased open the lid of the casket. Inside, a human form, wasted and skeletal, stared up at him. A large wooden stake had been driven through the chest cavity. Shuddering, he quickly shut the lid. A *real* vampire, he thought. An honest-to-goodness bloodsucking creature of the night. A vampire straight out of horror movies.

He spun in a slow circle, taking in the vast room of treasures. *It's like being a kid in a candy shop,* he thought. His eyes fell upon a device made of two metal canisters. *And having all the money in the world to spend,* he added. The label read: ANTI-GRAVITY JETPACK. A quick survey told Flynn that he was still alone. This was too good an opportunity to pass up.

He picked up the jetpack and examined it carefully. There had to be an "ON" button somewhere…

Flynn located what appeared to be the proper button and flicked the switch. The jetpack shuddered once, and began to float in mid-air.

"Very cool," he said. "Impossibly cool… I wonder what this button does…"

He flicked another switch. Before he could do more than blink, the jetpack leapt forward, a blur of white light and exhaust trails.

"Oh, no!" he cried. He ran after it, hoping that Judson was on a lunch break, a bathroom break, outside being mugged—anything but watching him try to chase down a runaway treasure.

Lady Luck, it appeared, was not with him,

because as he ran past a large shelf of text, he
noted Judson reading a text. The moment of distraction was enough to cause even more damage
as Flynn and the jetpack crashed into a shelf,
and through a wooden fence to land in a heap at
the feet of... he looked up in time to get a lick
on the face from the fabled Unicorn.

"Perfect," he muttered. "Just perfect."

Judson walked by, still reading, and said, "It
usually takes the new Librarian at least four
hours until they fire up the jetpack. It only took
you three. Congratulations." He bent down and
flicked the OFF button. The jetpack coughed a
couple of times and shut down.

Flynn stood up slowly, and looked, horri-
fied, at the shattered pieces of some treasure or
another scattered across the floor. He gathered
them carefully and turned to the shelf, where,
somehow, the placard had managed to stay in
place. Maybe it wouldn't be that bad.

The sign read: THE HOLY GRAIL.

Wow, the Holy Grail, Flynn thought. *The
Holy Grail?!* "I broke the Holy Grail on my first
day?!"

Judson raised an eyebrow. "Did you?"

The pieces in Flynn's hands began to vibrate, and he dropped them onto the shelf. They slid toward each other and reassembled themselves in seconds into a simple metal chalice.

"It takes a bit more than a knock to the floor to destroy a holy relic," Judson said. "The metal of the Grail has become brittle over the centuries, but nothing we know of can actually destroy it."

Flynn stared at the Grail, transfixed by the knowledge that the cup of Christ was real... sitting on a shelf in front of him... while nearby a Unicorn munched on oats, a vampire slept, and a jetpack waited only for some fool to turn it on. And more, so much more. He could spend his entire lifetime exploring the Library and not get through half of it. It was Paradise.

"You've been here all day, Flynn," Judson said. "Go home."

"All this'll still be here tomorrow, right?"

Judson laughed. "The Library opens tomorrow at seven. You can come back then."

Flynn looked at his watch, and Judson took him gently by the arm, leading him toward the elevator.

"Flynn, I believe in you. In time, I think there's a possibility you could become the best Librarian since Eldred the Truly Wonderful."

Judson pointed to a series of portrait paintings along the wall. Eldred was in a heroic pose, holding Pandora's Box in his arms. Other paintings ran in a sequence down the wall, depicting other Librarians.

Flynn scanned them—men and no few women who had collected the treasures of humanity and guarded them for centuries. Their names and faces were hidden from the public, the great services they performed went unrecognized, yet they were heroes.

"Eldred the Truly Wonderful," he said. "I'd settle for 'Flynn the Not Quite so Embarrassing and Rather Pleasant at Parties.'"

He strolled along the wall of paintings. The most recent showed an image of a dark-haired, charismatic-looking man. The date was recent.

"Edward Wilde," he read on the placard. "He must have been the last Librarian."

Judson nodded somberly. "May God rest his soul."

"I still don't understand," he said. "What exactly is the Library? Who were all these

Librarians? Is this a government agency?"

"The Library predates governments, Flynn. We are beholden to no one. The Librarians act and serve as the trustees. They serve, safeguard, and sacrifice in the name of all that is good and just."

"Ahh, the three 'S's'. Easy to remember."

"Funny," Judson said, clearly not amused. He turned and guided Flynn away from the paintings, steering him to the elevator once more and leaving him to ride to the top floor and go outside alone.

Stepping out into the last sunlight of the day, Flynn turned and looked back at the building that housed so many secrets and so much knowledge.

The university, all that schooling was just the beginning, he thought. This is where I truly belong.

Flynn got home to find his mom on a ladder, hanging up a gigantic banner that read: CONGRATULATIONS! He'd called her earlier in the day to let her know he'd gotten a job, and that he'd be home later. Pleased, he smiled up at her, and she climbed down the ladder, wrapped her arms around him, and kissed him soundly on the cheek.

"Hey!" he said.

"My baby got a job!" Margie beamed. "I thought it called for a celebration. I even made your favorite cake."

"You shouldn't have," Flynn said.

"This is a big day," she said. "So tell me, what's your new job? Sixteen years of college, all those fancy degrees... what are you doing?"

Thinking back to his day at the Library, Flynn once again felt that huge smile on his face. "I'm the Librarian," he said.

Flynn watched a variety of expressions chase each other across her face—expectant excitement, confusion, dismay, and perhaps a few other emotions as well.

"Librarian?" she said. "I mean—librarian! *Librarian?*"

She was obviously stunned. "No, no, you don't understand. This is the greatest job ever," Flynn said. "I've finally found my place."

"Sixteen years of college and you put books on shelves?" Before he could reply, she held up a hand. "No! It's good. You're good with the bookshelving."

"It's more than it sounds. A lot more. I'm not allowed to say how much more, but... if you knew, you'd be really impressed."

Margie shook her head, then smiled. "I *am* impressed. I'm your mother and I love you no matter what you do. I'm sure you'll be the best librarian ever. Now go get yourself a big piece of cake."

As Flynn headed for the kitchen, he heard her sigh and say, *"Librarian?"* He didn't respond, just smiled to himself and kept walking.

Judson was entering the last of the day's notes in his journal—beginning the chronicle, as it were, of Flynn Carson, the Librarian who was "Not Quite So Embarrassing and Rather Pleasant at Parties"—when he heard the noises coming from the back hall. Still chuckling at his new charge's antics, he moved the bookcase and walked down the hall toward the elevator leading to the Library.

The elevator doors were open! Judson ran forward, seeing the two armed guards lying on the floor. He knew they were dead before he got there, but knelt down to check anyway. His suspicions were correct, and Judson reached for the alarm, when two things happened at once.

A blinding pain shot through the back of his head.

Everything went dark.

The skyline of New York City at night was magnificent. A powerful neon illusion that the watcher knew disguised a great deal of crime and trash. It was one of the things he loved about the city. He continued to stare out the window, while two of the operatives he'd sent waited in silence behind him.

They bore a tattoo mark similar to his own, which ran along the back of his hand and up his arm: a serpent, multi-colored, with an open mouth full of fangs. The similarities between them all, however, ended there. He was in charge, and making them wait a moment would be a good test.

How long would it be before they spoke? Which of them would do so first? That would tell the watcher many things about them. He turned away from the window and studied them, maintaining his silence.

Finally, the male operative cleared his throat. It sounded like fear. But he didn't speak. That was telling.

The woman, who was called Lana, was the first to talk. "Everything went exactly as you said it would." She handed him a long, wooden shaft—part of a spear.

"After all that," the man, Rhodes, said, "do you want to tell us what we stole?"

The watcher stepped toward the operatives, his movements casual and slow; still, they flinched backward. Another telling bit of information about these two, he noted.

"What you stole is the realization of our five-thousand-year-old dream." Another step. "You'd think that would make me happy. At a minimum, pleased." With blinding speed, he reached out and grabbed Rhodes by the wrist with two fingers.

He twisted his grip slightly, and Rhodes let out a strangled garble of pain as he dropped to one knee. The watcher knew that the particular nerve cluster he'd grabbed was causing extreme agony.

"But as you can see," he continued, not releasing the man. "I'm *not* happy. *Not pleased.* Because you've only completed *half your mission.*"

Holding two hot coffees and jogging at the same time wasn't the best plan in the world, but Flynn gave the task his best shot. Charlene was walking up the steps to open the Library, and he wanted to get inside and resume his exploration of the treasures.

"It's 7:01 A.M.," he said as he caught up with her. "You'll have to dock your own pay."

Charlene's look would have scorched stone.

"Coffee?" Flynn asked, holding the cup out to her, and trying again to charm the woman.

She continued unlocking the doors. She opened them, then reached out and took the coffee. "I hate a kiss-ass," she said.

Flynn smiled and followed her inside, then headed for the secret hallway—only to come to a sudden halt, the smile twisting into a look of horror.

Judson's still form was lying on the floor.

"Charlene!" Flynn yelled as he ran to the fallen man. Judson groaned as Flynn helped him to his feet. "Are you all right?"

"They're not," Charlene said. Flynn turned to where she pointed, and spotted the two dead guards.

Wincing, Judson said, "Get me to my office. The surveillance tape."

Flynn and Charlene did as he asked, put a cold compress on his head, and gave him a glass of water. After resting for a minute, Judson struggled to his feet. Crossing the room, he removed several books from a shelf, revealing a television set. He tapped a few buttons on the remote control, and a surveillance tape from the hidden cameras in the building began to play.

They watched as the elevator doors opened and a team of commandos dashed into the security room. Dressed in matching black uniforms and carrying similar weaponry, they were obviously well-financed. Two silenced shots took out the guards. One of the commandos, an attractive woman with Asian features, quickly stepped to the hidden alarm panel and pressed the code to shut it off.

The glass doors slid open and the team rushed inside.

Judson pushed another button and the camera view changed to the inside of the Library of Unknown Sciences. The commandos rushed to a shelf and the woman grabbed what she wanted. As the others tried to get more of the treasures, she stopped them and began shoving them toward the exit. She glanced at her watch.

Judson stopped the videotape, freezing the image.

"They knew about the fail-safe," Charlene said. "They just had time to take one item."

Tapping a button, the image zoomed in on the woman's hand holding the object. Charlene gasped.

"They've taken the Spear of Destiny," Judson said. His voice was shaking.

Hitting another button, the screen shot was printed out. Judson looked at it briefly, then handed it to Flynn.

"You've heard of the Spear of Destiny?" Charlene asked.

Flynn nodded. "The Spear of Destiny is the spear that pierced the side of Jesus while he was on the Cross. An ancient talisman, reputed to have incredible powers. Legend holds that whoever possesses the Spear has the fate of the world in their hands."

"Precisely," Judson said. "For thousands of years, whoever has had the Spear, from Charlemagne to Napoleon, became the world's greatest conqueror."

Flynn studied the image. "But that's just a fragment of the Spear," he said.

"That's right," said Judson. "The Spear was far too powerful to keep intact. Since it can never be completely destroyed, hundreds of years ago, The Librarian broke it into three pieces. One piece has been kept in the Library. The other two were hidden in secret places elsewhere in the world."

"With the Spear broken up, is it still a threat?" Flynn asked.

"Hitler only had *one* of the pieces," Judson said. "Imagine the power of all three."

Flynn whistled. Judson restarted the videotape.

Back in the security room, the alarm lights were swirling, while the commandos raced for the door. One man, powerfully built, tried to hold the doors open for the others to exit. The doors finally slammed closed, tearing the sleeve from his coat.

"Freeze it there," Charlene said. "Zoom in."

Judson complied, and the image on the screen zeroed in on an image of a tattoo: a multi-colored serpent, open-mouthed, with protruding fangs. *"La Confrerie du Serpent,"* he whispered.

He suddenly stood, taking a book from a shelf. "Follow me," he said. He headed down a hallway, paging rapidly through the book.

"'The Serpent Brotherhood,'" Flynn translated. "Seriously? Do these guys play a lot of *Dungeons and Dragons?*"

"They were a splinter group," Judson answered. "Back when the Library was in Alexandria in ancient times. Then they called themselves the Brotherhood of the Serpent, but overtime the name changed, though their goals didn't. They were scholars too, but they wanted to use the powers of the artifacts to rule the world. They took their name from the Serpent who brought knowledge to Adam and Eve."

Stopping at a shelf, he pulled out an ancient book, and opened it to a page with a colorful illustration: two groups of scholars arguing and fighting over a glowing horde of treasure between them.

"Disagreement became hatred. Hatred became a secret war. It was the Serpent Brotherhood who incited the riot that led to the destruction of the first Library in the late fourth century."

"And they want the Spear... why?"

"For thousands of years, while the Library has sought knowledge, the Serpent Brotherhood has been seeking power," Judson said. "Power to control the world, reshape it as they see fit. The Spear could very well be the key that gives it to them." He replaced the book on the shelf and led the way back to Charlene's office.

"We'd better call the police," Flynn said.

Judson began rummaging in a large trunk behind Charlene's desk. He was tossing gear into a pile: bags, ropes, a backpack, an oilskin short-coat. Flynn picked up the phone and started to punch 9-1-1.

"Oh, yes," Charlene said. "Call the police. Tell them about the Spear of Destiny, the Golden Goose, the Lost Ark of the Covenant. You can even mention King Midas while you're at it."

Stopping in mid-dial, Flynn tried to come up with a snappy comeback—and failed.

"Enjoy your stay in the psych ward," Charlene continued. "I understand they're offering the Thorazine in a delicious vanilla flavor these days."

Judson finished putting the gear into the backpack. "No one can understand the mysteries of the Library unless they've experienced them," he said. He tossed the backpack to Flynn, who caught it awkwardly. "Only *you* can get the Spear piece back."

Flynn put the phone down, his mind trying to grasp what he was being told. "No," he said. "No, no, and nooooooo. There's got to be somebody more qualified."

"Accept your destiny, Flynn Carson," he said.

"I don't believe in destiny," he retorted.

"Is it coincidence that we've finally found a replacement Librarian just before this crisis? Coincidence that you're one of the most learned candidates we've ever had?" Judson said. "No. I don't accept that. Call it destiny, luck, even Chaos Theory if it pleases you, but you are the one for this task. You are the only one on Earth for it."

"And think of it this way," Charlene added. "If you make it back, you'll be a hero."

"Well, that's not..." Flynn started to say, then stopped. "What do you mean if I make it back?"

"It's not as bad as it looks," Judson said.

Flynn ignored him, and focused on Charlene. "When you said, 'If I make it—'"

"At least they didn't find the book," Judson interrupted. He grabbed an ancient text from Charlene's desk. "If you want to really hide something, do it in plain sight." He handed the book to Flynn. "This has all the clues you'll need to find the other two pieces before the Serpent Brotherhood. This book tells their locations." He paused, then frowned. "All we know for certain is that the second piece is somewhere in the Amazon jungle."

"That narrows it down to only three million square miles," Flynn said, his voice dripping with sarcasm. "A snap to find."

"You'll find your way," Judson reassured him. "The Librarian always does. Now you must go."

He took Flynn by the arm and began leading him out of the Library.

Charlene flanked him on the other side, and Flynn wondered if they were trying to keep him from running away. Ever curious, he opened the book Judson had given him. It was filled with strange symbols, somewhat similar to Egyptian hieroglyphics, but not the same. After a moment, he realized what the language was.

"This is written in the Language of the Birds," he said.

Judson nodded. "Mankind's universal language before God decided to have man speak many tongues after the fall of the Tower of Babel."

"Ummm… it's been a dead language for *thousands of years,*" Flynn said. "Nobody alive knows how to read it."

"Then you'd better get cracking on learning it," Charlene quipped. She handed him a sheaf of documents. "Here's your passport, along with what you'll need at the airport."

"How'd you manage that?" Flynn asked.

"We *are* the Library," she said simply.

Turning his attention back to the book, Flynn said, "Even with the Rosetta Stone, it took hundreds of Egyptologists seventeen years to decipher Egyptian hieroglyphics."

"You have considerably less time than they did," Judson said.

"It's only my second day on the job," Flynn protested. "I don't even have a parking space yet. I think you should have a parking space assigned before you get sent off to fight an evil conspiracy—"

"If the Serpent Brotherhood gets their hands on all three pieces, then the fight will be as good as over. Trust me, it will be horrible."

"But why pick me?" Flynn asked. "This is a terrible decision."

"The Library doesn't make terrible decisions, Flynn," Judson said. "Just remember one thing: The most valuable object in the world isn't in the Library." He pointed to Flynn's head. "It's right up there."

The enormity of the situation hit him, and he suddenly stopped walking. He looked at

Judson. "The fate of the world is in my hands,"
he said.

Judson nodded.

"That's just…" Flynn paused. "That's just so
sad."

He slung the backpack over his shoulder,
and went out the doors.

Shaking her head, Charlene looked at Judson.
"We're doomed. You know that right? He does-
n't have the experience to deal with this on his
own."

"Who says he'll be on his own?" Judson asked
her. "Send no one to lend him a hand and keep him
out of trouble. He'll do fine." He walked back
inside. "Oh, and come help me deal with the
bodies of the guards," he added. "I'm not going
to haul them off on my own."

"You're the boss," Charlene said, following
him in. "But I still say we're doomed."

CHAPTER FOUR

*I*t *could be worse,* Flynn thought as he struggled to get into his seat in business class. He glanced into the overcrowded coach cabin. *I could be flying back there.* He got into his seat and took out the ancient book Judson had given to him.

How in the world am I going to learn the Language of the Birds in a few hours?

As though summoned by the thought, the TV screen in front of him flickered to life, and an image of Judson appeared. "The book will give you clues to guide you to the hidden locations of the Spear pieces. Guard it with your life," he said. The image flickered once more and disappeared.

"That's amazing," Flynn muttered to himself, but then the image reappeared.

"One more thing I forgot to tell you," Judson said. "Trust *no one*. Good luck, Flynn." The image disappeared again.

"How'd you do that?" Flynn asked. He turned to the other passengers seated next to him. "That's so cool. Did you see that?"

From the looks they gave him, the others clearly hadn't seen it. They thought he was nuts.

Shrugging, Flynn turned his attention to the ancient book and began trying to learn a dead language.

Within a short time, he had filled page after page with his notes. The oldest known languages in the world gave clues about pronunciation. A "best guess" of how the language was spoken.

"The vowels," he said to himself, "are Akkadian, but the consonants are early Sumerian, Hebrew, and Inwewinan Indian." He consulted his notes again. "And the genders are Sanskrit, the phonemes are Etruscan, with some of the semantic features of Viteliu."

Feeling a heavy gaze, Flynn looked up to notice a heavy-browed, tough-looking man staring at him. "Sorry," he said. "Thinking out loud. Bad habit."

Just then, the curtains sectioning off business class from first class parted. Flynn felt his jaw unhinge and worked to bring it back up where it belonged. An absolutely beautiful woman was being escorted to her seat by the pilots. Throughout the section, male heads turned to watch her move down the aisle. Her steps and manner were confident, and flowed as though she were walking on air rather than trying to struggle down a narrow plane aisle.

"So nice of you to let me watch takeoff from the cockpit," she was saying to the pilots. "But honestly, I really should take my seat."

There was something about this woman, Flynn thought, that made her more than physically attractive. She had something… He shook his head, trying to put his finger on it. One of the pilots put her two bags into the overhead compartment.

"I was hoping to have the aisle seat," the woman said, staring pointedly at Flynn.

One of the pilots backed her up with a hard stare of his own. Flynn realized they meant him, and slid over to the window seat, trying to gather his papers as he went.

"I'll come visit later," the woman told the pilots. "I promise."

The pilots had the good grace to blush, and headed back up to the cockpit. Flynn finished gathering his papers and books, stacking them on his tray table.

"You won't believe this," he said, "but this is my first plane flight. You fly often?"

The woman turned to him and arched one finely detailed eyebrow. "Let us stop for a moment," she said, "and consider the following: I'm way out of your league. Way out. If your league were to explode, the sound of it would not reach *my* league for three days. So for everyone's sake, let's just enjoy a companionable silence."

"I see you have a healthy ego," Flynn quipped.

"If it's the truth," she said, "it ain't ego. Now, *shhh*. Enjoy the peanuts. They're salty."

Almost seven hours into the flight, and Flynn was beginning to feel real hope. His copious notes and papers were strewn everywhere, and he was thankful for all the time he'd spent studying ancient languages in college. The beautiful woman next to him sipped on her champagne—a very good brand, at that—while he continued to work.

He glanced down at the notes once more, and the keys suddenly clicked.

"I did it!" he cried. "Look at that! I learned the Language of the Birds! Not even a Rosetta Stone and I did it in—" he looked at his watch "—seven hours!"

The woman next to him offered a casual "whoppity-doo" glance.

"Sorry," Flynn said. "Go back to… being radiant."

She turned away, but Flynn continued to look at her, when that something different about her finally hit him. "The Golden Ratio—" he started to say, when she put a hand over his mouth.

"You're about to say that the ratio of 1.618-to-1 has been proven to be the key to everything in nature that we find beautiful, and that my face is the closest you've ever seen to this perfect ratio." She took her hand away.

"How could you possibly know that?" he asked.

"Because every geek I've ever met has tried to hand me that line," she said. Pointing to his papers, notes and books, she added, "And you are *clearly* a geek."

"Were you this dismissive and rude to all of them?" Flynn asked.

She smiled softly. "Geeks are a lot like wounded horses. It's kinder to put them down quickly."

The stewardess approached the woman. "The pilots would like you to join them in the cockpit," she said quietly. "To watch the sun rise over the rainforest."

"Of course they do," the woman said. She rose to her feet and followed the stewardess toward the front of the plane.

Taking the opportunity to use the restroom, Flynn got to his feet. "Of course they do," he muttered to himself. "Of *cooourse* they do…"

"That's The Librarian?" Rhodes asked, watching as Flynn worked his way toward the bathroom.

"Don't underestimate him," Lana said. "Now stay put for a moment."

Dressed in the uniform of a stewardess, she quickly worked her way up to first class, and leaned down to speak to a man seated there.

"Excuse me, sir," she whispered. "We have a problem. Are you the air marshal?"

The man nodded.

"Good to know," she said, driving a hypodermic needle into his neck with the speed and precision borne of practiced skill. He kicked out, once, then his eyes rolled back and he slumped in his seat, unconscious.

Flynn really had to go to the bathroom, so when the large man stepped in front of him, he tried to edge his way past. The man wouldn't move out of the way.

"Pardon me," Flynn said, "But I really need to get…"

At that moment, he noticed the man's tattoo: a multi-colored serpent, just like the one he'd seen in the surveillance video. Pleased, he said, "Hey!" before he realized that this was a *bad thing*.

"Oh, hey…" he said, his voice trailing off weakly.

The man shoved Flynn backward, and he crashed into another man, who grabbed his arms tightly. A quick glance down at the newcomer's hand revealed yet another serpent tattoo.

How many of these guys are there? Flynn wondered, scanning the rest of the section. His eyes widened as he realized that *everyone* in business class was staring at him—and *all of them* had the tattoo.

A man and a woman—the operatives he'd seen on the videotape—approached from the front of the section. Without a word, the man slammed a fist into Flynn's face, and he crumpled under the blow.

Reeling, Flynn looked up to see the woman taking out a huge hypodermic needle.

"Again," the man said, "I'm not impressed."

"This will make you tell us everything we need to know," the woman said, showing Flynn the needle. She grabbed his arm and started pushing his sleeve up.

Just as she was about to plunge the needle into his arm, the curtain separating business and first class flew open, and the beautiful woman he'd been sitting next to came flying into the section. A cultist moved forward to stop her, and faster than Flynn could follow, she grabbed his outstretched arm, twisted it around, shattered his elbow, and sent him staggering away. The man's scream was piercing.

Without any sign of real exertion, the woman tore through several more cultists. Bones were broken, shoulders dislocated, and in short, it looked to Flynn like a Jet Li movie. In mere seconds, the woman had closed to where Flynn was being held, leapt into the air, and delivered a crushing kick to the skull of the man who'd been holding him.

Flynn did the only reasonable thing he could do as the man's body flew forward. He ducked, which caused the cultist to slam into the woman holding the needle and the man who'd punched him in the face. The moment he was free, "Ms. Of Course They Do" grabbed Flynn by the arm and began rushing him back in the direction of their seats.

Behind him, the man who'd punched him in the face was yelling, "Get him! *Get him!*"

The attractive woman with the needle hissed, "I told you not to underestimate him!"

The sound of bodies being shoved in a small space, yells and curses was everywhere. As they reached their seats, the woman opened the overhead compartment and grabbed her two bags. Flynn snagged his backpack and the other belongings.

"Who are you?" he asked.

The woman glanced briefly at him. "I'd love to chat, but I really have to…" Her voice trailed off as she turned her attention back to the approaching cultists. With ninja-like speed, she began twirling her bags, whipping them about her head like a pair of nunchuks. Several thuds and groans followed her attack, and the thugs fell into the aisle, blocking it.

"Follow me," the woman said, turning and heading toward first class. Flynn stayed right on her heels, stepping out of the way when she paused in the kitchen galley and pushed two large food carts into the aisle.

"Keep going!" she said, shoving him forward to the front of the plane. Everyone in first class stared at them like they'd lost their minds, the commotion behind them growing louder.

"Who are you?" Flynn repeated.

"The woman who's trying to save your pitiful life," she answered. "And it's Nicole."

He smiled. "Oh. Well, I'm—"

"I know who you are," she interrupted. She glanced at the flight monitors near the exit door of the plane, smiled—and *opened the emergency exit!*

Furious winds whipped into the plane, and passengers began screaming in terror.

"What the hell are you doing?" Flynn yelled.

"We're going out," she said, strapping one of her two bags onto her back.

Flynn realized they were parachutes, and she fully intended for them to jump out of this plane. He stared out through the open door.

"Don't tell me you're afraid of heights," she said.

"No," Flynn said. "It's just that I know the odds of an untrained guy like me surviving a jump from 10,000 feet at this speed is seven to two against!"

The woman smiled at him, and Flynn thought again how pretty she was.

Then she shoved him out of the plane—without his parachute!

"What are the odds now?" Nicole shouted as she watched Flynn hurtle toward the jet engine, just missing it. *What a geek,* she thought. *He's no Edward Wilde, that's for sure.*

Behind her, the two thugs who'd been getting ready to torture information out of Flynn burst into the cabin.

"There!" one of them shouted, spotting her.

She smiled, saluted gamely, and jumped.

Below, she caught sight of Flynn, flailing helplessly in the air as he hurtled toward the ground. Arching her approach toward him gracefully, she swooped down upon him, and caught him in her arms.

"Hold on tight," she said, "and you might just live."

Well, she thought, *he was at least following instructions. He's holding on tight.* Wincing, she added to herself. *Very tight.*

She pulled the cord and tried to ignore his scream of surprise, then began guiding their slow descent into the Amazon.

"Don't look down," she said.

The sun chose that moment to rise, offering the canopy of the Amazon, a gorgeous cloak of red and orange hues.

Flynn clutched her tighter. "I think I'm going to be sick," he mumbled.

Lana stared out the window at the parachute floating gently toward the jungle below, then turned to Rhodes. "He brilliantly lowers our expectations and then jumps without a chute. He's quite… remarkable." Not only was he cute, Lana thought, but well, very exciting.

Ignoring her tone, Rhodes pulled out a cell phone and punched in a number. There was a long moment of silence, then he said, "They got away."

Lana watched as her partner's eyes went wide with fear. "Yes, sir!" Rhodes said. "I promise I won't fail again, sir! Thank you, sir!" He flipped the phone closed and put it away.

Obviously terrified at whatever he'd been told, Rhodes looked at her and said, "We've *got* to get that book."

If Flynn had been given a choice about where to land, the middle of the Amazon wouldn't have been high on the list. Still, the woman did an admirable job guiding them through the dense trees to a small clearing, and they landed in a rough heap.

Flynn rolled away from her and the chute, then grabbed a branch on the ground and brandished it as a club—though having seen how easily she dispatched the cultists, he had plenty of doubts about its effectiveness as a weapon against her.

"Who the *hell* are you?!" he asked again.

The woman stood gracefully and stepped out of the chute cords. "Don't get your panties in a bunch, junior. Judson told me to watch out for you."

"Judson told me to trust no one," Flynn said.

The woman removed a badge from her pocket and tossed it to him. She began rolling up the chute. "*I'm* no one," she said. "The name's Nicole Noone." She smiled. "Cool, huh?"

Flynn raised an inquisitive eyebrow. "You mean it's pronounced 'no one' instead of 'noon'?"

Nicole glared at him. "That a problem for you?"

"No," he said quickly. "No problem at all." He handed back the badge.

"Didn't they tell you to expect me?" she asked.

"They didn't tell me anything," Flynn muttered, tossing down the branch. "I have no idea what I'm doing."

"Really?" Nicole said.

Flynn pulled out his cell phone, but before he could punch in a number, Nicole stopped him. "No calls," she said. "They'll use the signal to triangulate our position. They'll be here soon enough—no point in helping them along."

"That's against the law," he said.

Nicole opened her remaining bag and removed a large leather sheath, which she strapped to her leg. "Let's see," she said. "They just attacked and tried to kill you on a public plane. Do you really think they're worried about FCC regulations against phone-tapping?"

"They didn't try to kill me," Flynn pointed out. "They just wanted to inject me with sodium pentothal so I'd tell them where I hid the book."

Nicole opened Flynn's backpack and pulled out the ancient book. "Who'd have thunk it?" she said.

"If you want to really hide something," he said, "do it in plain sight."

Nicole pulled a large machete from her bag and slid it into the sheath on her leg.

"Wow," Flynn said. "How'd you get *that* on the plane? Me, they took away my nose hair clippers."

Nicole smiled, then glanced around the thick jungle. "Where the hell are we?" she asked.

"How should I know?" Flynn replied. "You pushed me out of the plane, remember?"

"You're the brains of this operation," she said. "You figure it out."

"You think I can't?" Flynn asked. "I could just climb that tree and in a matter of seconds I'd know precisely where we are."

The woman cocked an eyebrow, gestured widely at the tree, and said, "I'm not stopping you."

Flynn walked over to the nearest tree and examined it carefully. He hadn't done a lot of tree-climbing in his youth. He glanced back at the woman, but her gaze was both unhelpful and skeptical.

Grasping the trunk firmly, he managed several inches before his attempt to impress the woman was cut short by him sliding back down and tearing his shirt.

"Need some help?" she asked.

"I'm fine," he said, doing his best to ignore her quiet snorts of laughter.

"You go get 'em, monkey boy."

Flynn tried again. And again. But each attempt only led to him slipping down and scratching himself on the rough bark. Still, he wasn't ready to give up—especially not with the Princess of Power watching and laughing at him.

"Your husband must be the tree climber in the family," she snickered.

"Attacking my masculinity," Flynn said. "Very helpful." He took a deep breath and somehow managed to get up into the tree. The woman climbed up behind him and they reached the top without anymore problems.

The early morning sun was still staining the sky when Flynn looked out over the treetops that stretched away into the remote distance. Smiling at the awe-inspiring sight, he took careful stock of the area.

"Let's hear it, genius," Nicole said. "Where are we?"

Obviously, the gorgeous sunrise and setting were warming her heart, Flynn thought. "Okay… well…" He pointed to a bird flying in the distance. "That's an extremely rare Blue Condor. It's only found within a hundred-mile radius of the Amazon's Purus Tributary." He scanned the horizon, noting a distant mountain. "The only mountain high enough to have a snowpack at this time of year at that elevation is Mount Porto Velho." Flynn paused, calculating in his head, then nodded. "That anthodite rock formation over there is Bolivar Rock. See how it looks like a profile of Simon Bolivar?"

Nodding once to himself, he said, "We're at 5.2° Latitude and 64.6° Longitude. Our destination is 5.4° Latitude and 64.9° Longitude—south and west, respectively." Flynn grinned at her.

"English!" Nicole snapped.

"Oh. Well, we need to go 27.4 miles that way," he said.

Nicole started down the tree and Flynn followed after her. "How'd you do that?" she asked.

"Basic geography, biology and botany," he said. Then, reluctantly added, "And I've kind of memorized the Earth."

She stopped climbing and looked up at him. "You're kidding."

"I like maps," Flynn said defensively.

"Maps my butt," she said. "You need to get out more." She continued her descent.

Following her, Flynn mumbled, "*Everyone* keeps telling me that."

CHAPTER FIVE

W*hack! Whack! Whack!* A brief grunt of exertion. *Whack! Whack! Whack-whack!*

Flynn tried to duck as another vine went winging over Nicole's head and directly into his face. The woman was not just good at breaking bones, but was hell on the local fauna, too. He tried to duck again, missed, and the vine slammed into his shoulders, nearly knocking him to the ground.

"You always travel with a machete?" Flynn asked, hoping she'd pause in her rapid destruction of the plant life long enough to answer— and give him a breather.

"I'm well prepared," she said.

"And, just maybe, a violent sociopath."

She *did* pause then, turned and smiled. "You say the sweetest things," she said. Then she returned to her work.

Noting a plant he wasn't familiar with, Flynn picked it up and stuffed it into his pack. "How many miles have we walked?" he asked. "Five? Ten?"

Nicole laughed. "Maybe one," she said. Her machete sang in the morning air, cleaving a path through the trees and vines.

Examining plants as they went, Flynn wished they had more time. He'd memorized numerous botany texts, but many of these plants were new to him—which meant, in all likelihood, that they would be new to the world. He paused to study one particularly eye-catching specimen when another vine slammed into him, this time knocking him right on his ass.

Catching his breath, he said, "Unknown plant phylum! I can't believe it. If you're nice, I'll name it after you."

She paused again, and said, "Be still my heart."

"Yeah," Flynn muttered under his breath. "We can call it Ficus Narcissus." He stuck the

plant into his pack with the others he'd taken,
brushed off his hands and stood… just in time
to catch another vine in the face.

It was going to be, he realized, a very, very
long day.

Lana enjoyed the finer things in life: good
champagne, handsome, intelligent men, a tough
fight won. Riding in a jeep over incredibly
tough terrain was definitely not on that list. Her
bumps and bruises had bumps and bruises—some
of them in spots best left unmentioned. Tearing
through the Amazon jungle with Rhodes, some
local cult members, and a tracker, left a lot to be
desired—especially when the trek didn't involve
using roads.

Finally, the jeep burst through one more
ridge of rocks and vines and into a small clearing. Rhodes and the others immediately got out,
and Lana gingerly followed them, rubbing her
aching muscles.

"This the place?" she asked.

Rhodes looked around the area carefully, then stepped toward a jumble of rocks and pulled a rolled-up parachute from beneath them. "This is it," he said. "It's a damn good thing our ground spotters saw them come in. We haven't lost that much time."

He turned to the tracker—a native of the region—and handed him the parachute. "You're supposed to be the best tracker in the Amazon," he said. "Get tracking."

Lana watched as the nimble little man studied the clearing, then scurried up a nearby tree. He came back down holding a piece of cloth.

"Isn't that the same color as the shirt the Librarian was wearing?" she asked.

Rhodes nodded. "Sure enough," he said.

The tracker studied the cloth a moment longer, then looked around the clearing. He pointed and headed into the jungle—leaving the others to decide if they were going to follow him or not. Assuming the tracker knew where he was going, and considering the alternative of getting back in the jeep, Lana followed on his heels.

Besides, she thought, the sooner we catch up, the sooner I'll see him again.

Hot, sweaty, and utterly miserable, The Librarian continued to follow her. He had a sort of persistent charm, Nicole thought... but he was still a geek. She continued forging the path while behind her, he talked and talked, and just when she thought he might be talked out, he'd start up again on a different subject. She had to give him credit for one thing: he *knew* a lot. The man was damn smart.

The problem was that she'd stopped listening quite some time ago. Tuning back in, she tried to focus on what he was saying, while at the same time, hacking through the plants and keeping one eye out for any danger.

"In the world of books, anything is possible," Flynn was saying. "I guess that makes me a dreamer. My mother says that my father was a dreamer. He died when I was a kid. Maybe I've subconsciously tried to make up for his absence by being as much like him as I could." There was a pause, then he added, "Wow! Can you believe I never realized that before?"

Not wanting to encourage him, Nicole stopped and without turning around said, "I'm sorry. Did you say something, cupcake?"

"I just figured that since we're going to be spending lots of time together we might as well get to know each other."

Nicole sighed and turned to face him. "You seem like the observant type," she said.

Spotting yet another plant that apparently intrigued him, Flynn pulled it from the ground and put it in his pack with the numerous others he carried. "I like to think so," he said.

"Good," she said. "Then you must have observed that I'm not the type who's suddenly going to open up to you." She paused, then added, "Right?"

"How long have you been working for the Library?" Flynn asked.

Shoulders sagging, Nicole said, "And yet you keep on trying."

Flynn smiled, and Nicole realized that the banter and the little breaks were probably all that were keeping him on his feet. He looked ready to drop. "I want to get to know the Nicole below the surface arrogance. Peel back the layers."

"And what do you think is under the surface arrogance?" she asked him.

"More arrogance," he said. "And then, maybe, some delicious layers of flaky disdain, all around a creamy sweet center of homicidal rage."

Nicole turned her back on him, her fist tight around the handle of the machete. Would it be doing the Library a favor to kill this annoying man? "*What* do I have to do," she pleaded, "to get you to shut up?"

"Okay, okay," Flynn said. "I promise I won't ask you any more questions."

Nicole sighed with relief.

"How long have you been working for the Library?" Flynn asked.

Unable to help herself, Nicole started to laugh. *Oh, to hell with it,* she thought. *He* can *be cute.* "Five years," she said.

"Uh-huh," he said. "And do these sort of jumping-out-of-a-plane, tree-climbing, hacking-through-the-jungle-adventure things always happen to you?"

"Yes," she said.

"I've got to admit I liked them way more in books," he said.

"Books?"

"Yes, the 'choose your own adventure' type books. I read a lot of them when I was about four."

"You'd rather *read* about an adventure than actually *have* one?" she asked.

"Umm… yes. No. I don't know," Flynn admitted.

"A regular hero," she said.

"Speaking of heroes," Flynn said, "I've been meaning to ask you. What happened to the last Librarian?"

The question hit her all wrong. Nicole knew that. But it didn't stop her reaction. She wheeled away from him. "Look, you don't need to know about me. I don't need to know about you. We just need to work together."

She started hacking away at the jungle again, angry at having been reminded of Edward Wilde.

"So…" Flynn said behind her. "Nothing good then."

"That's *not* a bridge," Flynn said, staring at the rickety-looking wooden slats that crossed over a gorge. He leaned forward and looked down. The drop was an easy thousand feet, maybe more. Nearby, a raging waterfall tore down a wall of rock.

"It's the only way across," Nicole pointed out.

Flynn pointed. "The support barrings have decomposed, and the wood has rotted. It's too damp here. Structurally, it can't possibly support our weight. Hence, it's *not* a bridge—it's a death trap."

Nicole stepped out onto the first slat of the bridge, the board creaking beneath her feet.

The woman isn't homicidal, Flynn thought. *She's suicidal.* He put out a hand, catching her shoulder. "You'll die," he said.

She pulled away from him, taking several more steps onto the so-called bridge, then held out a hand to him. "Take a chance, big boy," she said.

Shaking his head, Flynn stepped onto the bridge. This was crazy and they were both going to die. He took Nicole's hand, and they slowly began to work their way across.

"Just don't look down," she said.

Unable to stop himself, Flynn looked into the deep gorge—and froze in place. "Why do I always do that?" he asked.

Nicole squeezed his hand. "Do you trust me, Flynn?" she asked him.

"No," he said.

"Good," she said. "Focus on something else."

"You mean other than my impending death on the watery rocks below after a plummet of a thousand feet?"

"Yes," she said. "You must have a girlfriend of some sort back home, right? Big, horn-rimmed glasses, dirndle skirt, makes you watch a lot of subtitled documentaries on TV?"

"I'm… between girlfriends at the moment," Flynn answered.

"I suspected as much," Nicole said.

Flynn started to look down again, but Nicole grabbed him by the chin and forced him to look straight ahead. *"Focus,"* she said. "Have you figured out where the second piece is yet?"

Carefully putting one foot in front of the other, Flynn tried to pay attention to her questions and not the poor condition of the bridge. "I have a basic idea," he admitted. "But I'm not exactly sure. Most of the clues are pretty self-explanatory, except for this one: 'To get inside you must know the time it takes a bird to become a bird again.'" He glanced at Nicole, "Any idea what that means?"

"Here's how this works," she said. "You: brains. Me: brawn. Got it?"

Suddenly, a plank split beneath his feet with a loud cracking sound. Flynn felt his foot go through the bridge, his gaze riveted on the fall he was going to take, as yet another board crumbled beneath him. There was a disorienting, ride-in-the-elevator lurch in his stomach, and then he was falling.

He hitched in his breath to scream when his arms were nearly pulled from their sockets. Nicole had snatched him by the forearms as he fell. Hanging in space, Flynn looked down at the river below, and swallowed past the lump in his throat. Trying not to look too desperate and knowing he'd failed miserably, he stared up at Nicole.

Slowly, she pulled him back up onto the bridge. Once he was safely on his feet, she said, "There. Now that wasn't so bad, was it?"

"I hope you're having fun," he said.

"Actually," she said, grinning. "I am."

That was when the entire bridge lurched beneath them. A section of it dropped several feet with a loud thud as it came down on the supports.

Teetering with the motion, Flynn stared at Nicole. "Not good," he said.

A loud crack split the air. Torn between wanting to run and not wanting to move, both of them stayed motionless. Another crack, and the last supports gave way.

The bridge began to collapse.

"Run!" Nicole barked.

Flynn didn't need to be told twice. He and Nicole sprinted along the boards, feeling the collapsing sections get closer and closer. "I told you the bridge couldn't support us!" he shouted, jumping over a missing plank.

"Shut up and keep running!" she said.

Just as the final planks were coming apart at their heels, both of them jumped into the air, desperate to clear the last few feet. Flynn saw the ground come up to meet him, as Nicole landed in a heap beside him. Behind, the last pieces of the bridge fell into the gorge, crashing against the rocks on the way down.

Gasping for breath, Flynn simply laid there for a moment, grateful to be alive. "Wow," he said.

He struggled to his feet, noting a colorful Macaw flying overhead. Then more of the beautiful birds flew past on their way to a mineral rich clay lick. "The Macaw Clay Lick," he said. "Our next clue."

Nicole got to her feet. "See? Everything worked out perfectly."

Ignoring her, and the stabbing fear that she'd *enjoyed* their brush with a plummeting, watery death, he pulled out the book and began reading it. "I remembered correctly," he said. "From here, we just add up the first five numbers in Pi and go that many yards this way." He pointed to show which direction.

When Nicole didn't immediately respond, Flynn looked up and saw that she was staring at his feet. A horrible, itchy sensation began working up his leg. "That's... that's got to be something extremely poisonous, isn't it?" he asked. His voice was a hoarse whisper.

"Stay perfectly still," Nicole said. "Slowly pull down your pants. I'll yank it out."

Unable to help himself, and despite his terror, Flynn grinned.

"The *spider*," Nicole said.

"It'll bite you," he said.

"Your life is more important than mine," she countered. "Now do what I told you."

Flynn gingerly undid his pants and was glad they were loose-fitting khakis. He held them away from his waist, and then let them drop to the ground at his ankles, making certain they didn't brush the... *gigantic, hairy spider now crawling up his thigh!* The urge to scream was almost unendurable.

With amazing speed, Nicole grabbed the spider, which immediately bit her. She threw it away, but the damage was done. The effects of the toxins were already visible.

Nicole sat down at the base of a tree, shivering. Pulling his pants back up, Flynn rushed to her side.

He took her hand and examined the bite, then looked at the spider crawling away. "It's a Brazilian Wandering Spider," he said. "Sometimes they're called Banana Spiders."

"How poisonous?" she asked.

"It's one of the most deadly in the world," Flynn admitted.

"Crap," she said.

Flynn turned his attention back to the bite. Nicole began to shiver uncontrollably beside him—the venom was moving quickly. "Hold your arm down," he ordered. "It'll slow the venom—at least a little. The muscles in your lungs are starting to contract. Soon, they'll close up completely and you'll suffocate."

Nicole grasped his hand. "You have to keep going…"

"No…" Flynn said.

"You're The Librarian," she said, her voice determined. "You're more important—"

Flynn shook his head. "This is the Amazon," he said. "There's got to be a cure here somewhere."

He yanked his backpack off and upended the contents on the ground. Numerous plants he had collected fell into a pile. Rummaging through them, Flynn talked to himself. "Only five plant phylum contain the cure for the Wandering Spider bite. Three of them are indigenous to Asia, one to Africa, and one here: *Disaperium Firius.*"

Nicole slumped over, barely conscious.

"Damn it," Flynn swore, digging through the plants desperately. "Come on, come on," he urged himself. "I'm sure I put a *Disaperium Firius* in here!"

He picked up plants, glanced, then tossed them aside. "*Oxalis Regnelli. Strobilanthes Dyerionus. Tradescantia Pallida.* But no *Disaperium Firius!* Think, damn it! There must be something else that will work."

Noting that Nicole's breathing was becoming more ragged and shallow by the second, Flynn tore through the plants he'd collected a second time. Then it hit him, "*Ophrys Sphegodes!*" he said. "It might work!"

He only had one, so he took the time to carefully remove the plant's sepal, then forced it into Nicole's mouth, cradling her head in his arms.

"Swallow!" Flynn ordered her. "Come on, just breath once, let the neurostimulant react…" It was a long shot at best, but it was the only chance she had.

Several long seconds passed before Nicole took in a ragged breath, then another, and began coughing. Her eyes opened.

"It worked!" Flynn crowed. "I saved you." He wrapped his arms around her, hugging her tightly.

"Don't get too worked up about it," Nicole muttered.

"I'll take *that* as a thank you," he said.

Without warning, she grabbed a knife from her belt, aiming it at Flynn.

"Wait!" he yelled. "You're… you're delirious! Nicole, *don't*—"

She hurled the knife, sailing it past his ear—and into the spider behind him, pinning it to a nearby tree. Her strength was coming back, it seemed. She slowly got to her feet, though her legs were still a bit wobbly.

She tried to glare at him, but her woozy voice softened the overall effect. "You jeopardized the mission. You almost got yourself killed.

Again. From now on, you do exactly what I say. If I say, 'Stick a knife into your chest,' you ask, 'How far?' Nothing is more important than the mission. *Nothing* is more important than you finding the Spear!"

She stumbled away from him and over to the spider, pulling out her knife and replacing it in the sheath. The spider splatted to the ground, and Nicole stormed off in the direction Flynn had indicated earlier.

He stared after her, silent at her rebuke.

It was only when she was sheltered by the dense trees, her whole form nothing more than a vague outline, that she said anything else. Quietly, her voice came back to him, "Thank you."

Flynn smiled. "You're welcome," he said. Then he headed off after her into the jungle, sparing one final glance at the nasty creature that had almost killed them both, now lying dead.

CHAPTER SIX

L ana stared into the gorge, noting the broken pieces of wood that had once been a bridge on the watery rocks below. "Did they make it across?" she asked the tracker.

Their guide pulled out a set of binoculars and peered across to the other side of the chasm. A long moment of quiet—the only sounds the distant cries of birds—was followed by a sharp nod. Lana wasn't surprised—this Librarian was obviously up to the task.

She looked at Rhodes. "So, now what?" she asked. "We're obviously not using the bridge."

"Nope," he said, digging into his pack. "We're using this." He held up a long, tube-like object that resembled a gun, with a grappling hook and long line protruding from the end. "I'll fire this across, and we'll go over in harness."

Lana looked down into the gorge again. "Oh," she said. Not wanting to show fear, but nonetheless afraid, she said, "There isn't another bridge?"

The tracker shook his head. "Two, maybe three days lost."

"Perfect," she said sarcastically.

"We can't afford to lose two or three days," Rhodes said. "*He'll* kill us both."

Lana nodded in reluctant agreement. "Don't miss," she said. "Whatever you do. We've only got one shot at this."

Rhodes stepped to the edge of the gorge and took careful aim at a cluster of rocks on the far side. He paused, and made a slight adjustment for the arc of descent, as well as the winds billowing up from the gorge.

"Hope like hell this works," he muttered, and pulled the trigger.

The grappling hook burst out of the tube with a deep thrumming sound and shot across the gorge. The line it carried trailed behind it, whipping in the wind.

"Go," Rhodes whispered in encouragement.

The hook landed on the cluster of rocks, and, using brute force, Rhodes yanked on the line.

Lana let out a sighing breath of relief. The grapple had set deep into the rocks. "Whew!" she said. The slide across the gorge wouldn't be fun, given her fear of heights, but losing time, coupled with the threat their boss represented, scared her a hell of a lot more.

Rhodes connected the line to a heavy-trunked tree, knotting it carefully. "Who wants to go first?" he asked, sounding cheery. "Lana?"

"I can't wait," she muttered under her breath. She took a harness system from him and began strapping it on. She hoped by going first that the line would be stronger—after several people, heavier men in particular, had gone across, it might be weaker.

Once she was strapped in, Rhodes walked with her to the edge of the chasm and helped hook her to the line. "I'll go last," he said, keeping his voice low. "Better to make sure these locals don't decide to take a vacation and leave us on the other side."

"Good idea," Lana said, noting the looks of fear on the other men's faces.

"Have fun," he said, then gave her a solid shove off the edge.

It took all her willpower not to scream as she began to pull herself over the gorge, and the thousand-foot drop beneath her.

Rhodes was almost across the gorge when his cell phone rang. Distracted, he actually let go of the line for a moment, hanging there in space and reaching to answer it, before he realized what a bad idea that was. Ignoring its shrill call, he finished traversing the last fifteen feet, and Lana helped him get to his feet, then unhooked him from the harness. Nearby, the tracker was already examining the area.

The phone rang again, and this time Rhodes answered. "Yes, sir." There was a pause and then, "Sorry, sir, I was hanging from a grappling line with a thousand-foot drop beneath me." Another pause. "No, sir, I'm not trying to be a smartass." Rhodes looked at Lana and rolled his eyes. "Yes, sir," he said. "We'll get it soon, sir… I know the consequences."

He clicked the phone shut. "Damn wanker," he said. He turned to Lana. "We'd *really* better get that book."

The tracker came over, holding a very large, very dead spider and a handful of plants. "She got bit by a Brazilian Wandering Spider, and he saved her with an *Ophrys Sphegodes* plant. Smart man—only the natives of this area even know it works."

"Ophrys Sphegodes?" Lana asked.

"Spider Lily," the tracker said.

"Then what?" Rhodes demanded.

"They yelled at each other for a bit and then they left that way—" he gestured with his head "—about an hour and seventeen minutes ago."

"We're gaining on them, then," Rhodes said.

The tracker nodded and headed into the jungle.

"He's very good," Lana said, with a touch of awe in her voice.

Rhodes couldn't help but wonder if she meant the tracker.

Nicole's strength had returned, though it had been slow going at first. Flynn felt more confident than he ever had before in his life—he'd saved her from certain death. Maybe he was cut out to be The Librarian, after all.

"So," he asked, "what do you do for fun?"

"I can kill a man fifty-seven different ways," she said. Her voice was cheerful, as though the prospect of demonstrating all fifty-seven of them had just crossed her mind.

"That's good," he said with a trace of sarcasm. "Let it free. The sensitive soul inside of you that's so desperate to come out." A beautiful tree—bright red and almost glowing— stopped him in his tracks.

"Flynn," Nicole said, "you may know just about everything in the world, but you have no idea, none at all, about what sets my soul free."

He nodded solemnly at her, bent down, and picked up a fist-sized rock. "You're probably right," he said, then turned and tossed the rock into the tree.

Thousands of red-morpho butterflies leapt into the air, revealing that they were the reason for its coloring. They swarmed over the area, several of them landing on him and Nicole. She lifted a hand in wonder and a butterfly gently landed on her finger.

Flynn smiled and continued on. Behind him, he felt Nicole watching him, and heard her say, in a voice that wasn't meant to be heard, "Well, I'll be damned. The geek's got game."

He didn't say a word, but his smile got quite a bit bigger.

The fire wasn't much, but it at least provided some warmth. They were high enough that once the sun went down, the temperature dropped rapidly. Nicole turned the spit over the fire, letting the animal cook a minute more. When it was done, she removed the spit from the flames and used her knife to divide the meal.

Flynn took the offered food, but said, "Okay, so *why* won't you tell me what it is?"

She arched an eyebrow. "Because I'll tell you, you'll get all cheeky, and refuse to eat. We'll argue, finally you'll take a bite and say it tastes just like chicken. So, please, save us the drama and just eat it."

Grinning, Flynn took a bite. "Tastes just like chicken," he said around a mouthful.

Nicole ate in silence, since any response was likely to get him going. She watched as he studied the book with care. He was more studious than Edward Wilde had been, more cautious in ascertaining knowledge.

"'To get inside you must know the time it takes a bird to become a bird again,'" he said, quoting the passage that had him stumped. "It's got to be some sort of metaphor. What does the bird stand for?"

"What kind of bird?" Nicole asked. "Like a phoenix?"

Flynn considered this. "Maybe," he said. "According to legend, the phoenix lived for 500 years before bursting into flames, only to be reborn from its own ashes."

"There you go," Nicole said. "The answer is 500 years."

Flynn thought for a moment, then said, "Maybe… no, I don't think so. It doesn't feel quite right. From a literary point of view, the bird usually stands for achieving unattainable heights, maybe like some mountain…" His voice trailed off as he continued to ponder. "I have no idea," he finally said. "Maybe I'm not as smart as I think I am."

Moving so fast he didn't see it coming, Nicole reached out and slapped him across the face, hard enough to get his attention.

"What the hell was that for?" he asked, rubbing the spot on his cheek where she'd connected.

"I won't let anybody talk about the Librarian like that. Not even The Librarian," she said.

Flynn laughed. "A simple warning would have done just fine," he said, rising to his feet.

"Where are you going?" she asked.

He nodded toward the foliage. "You, by chance, don't have any toilet paper, do you?"

She smiled and handed him a broad leaf. "Knock yourself out."

Taking the leaf with reluctance, Flynn turned and headed into the jungle.

Nicole smiled and shook her head. *A total geek,* she thought, *but he* does *have his uses…*

He whistled softly from the brush, and Nicole moved through the trees to join him. *Hope he's not looking for help wiping himself...* she thought, grimacing.

"What's up?" she said when she arrived on the scene.

Flynn pointed, and she looked over the edge of the cliff they'd tackled that day. At the base of the cliff was a small campfire.

"Serpent Brotherhood," she said. "They're moving faster than I thought."

"Do you think they saw us?" he asked.

"It's unlikely," she said. "The angle's wrong. But better safe than sorry." She headed back to the fire and Flynn followed. She put out the fire, covering the embers with dirt.

"Do we go or stay?" he asked.

"They wouldn't dare do that climb in the dark. They'll wait till morning." She grinned. "You can go to the bathroom safely."

"Funny, I've lost the urge," Flynn said.

Without the fire, the temperature on top of the cliff was very cold. In a short time, both of them were shivering.

"The windchill factor," he said to her. "We *could* get hypothermia unless we do something drastic."

"Could," she said. "This is where you tell me that the only way we can survive is by huddling together for body warmth."

"Well, if you insist," Flynn said, shrugging.

Nicole glared at him, but the idea of being warmer was hard to refuse. She motioned and he sat down next to her on the ground. They wrapped their arms around each other. "Body warmth *only,*" she said. "Got it?"

Snuggling closer, Flynn said, "Got it."

After a few minutes, they both felt quite a bit warmer. The sky was clear, the stars brilliant white against the black sky.

"Cassiopeia, Fheliak, Terebellum, Andromeda," Flynn said, noting the constellations.

"Let me guess," Nicole said. "You've memorized the universe."

"The *known* universe," he replied. "It's a big place."

She shook her head. "Is there anything you *don't* know?" she asked.

He didn't answer for a bit, probably trying to work up the nerve to ask his question.

"Nicole?" he finally said.

"Hmm?"

"There's lots of things I don't know, but one thing I don't know for certain."

"What's that?" she asked.

"What happened to the last Librarian?" Flynn asked. "I've got a right to know."

"He died," she answered shortly. "End of story. I'm not keen on remembering details."

"You're the type that remembers everything," he said.

"You don't know anything about me," Nicole said. "Nothing."

"Really?" Flynn asked. "You're the youngest of three siblings, the only girl. Your father is British, but your mother is South American—Argentinean, to be specific, but you never bothered to learn Spanish. You grew up behaving like a tomboy, but you secretly loved the romance novels of Danielle Steele."

Nicole's jaw dropped open as he continued. "You've never had any pets, your favorite stone is jade, and more than anything, you wish you could forget half of what you've seen." He paused, then concluded, "But you can't."

Trying to hide her stunned reaction to his dead-on assessment, Nicole said, "So what? I could do the same thing about you."

Flynn nodded. "Okay. Take your best shot."

Nicole stared at him, sizing him up, considering, then said, "Nerd."

He sat there for several long seconds, but when he apparently realized nothing more was forthcoming, he laughed. "Fair enough," he said.

She smiled and stood up, thinking about his earlier question. "The last Librarian," she said. "Edward Wilde."

"Yes," he said.

"Edward was... amazing," Nicole said. "Handsome, charming, absolutely brilliant, though not as studious, I think, as you are. I spent two years working with him. Two incredible years. He taught me about art, and I taught him how to fence. He'd teach me about poetry, and I'd instruct him in Tae Kwan Do." Her voice quieted, lost in the memory of him.

"He wasn't just smart," she added. "He was kind, generous. And when he looked at you, he looked right into your soul." She stopped and turned to face Flynn. "I did   the one thing I'm not supposed to do in my job."

"Enjoy someone's company?" Flynn asked.

"Hardly," she said. "I fell in love with him. And because of that, he's dead."

"Because of love?" he asked. "That's—"

"We were in the Antarctic," she said, interrupting him. "We slept together in an igloo he'd built, but when I awoke in the morning, he wasn't there. I ran outside just in time to see the Serpent Brotherhood cutting off his head."

"Jesus," Flynn whispered.

"I had one job," Nicole said. "Protect The Librarian. And I failed."

He reached for her then, putting a hand on her shoulder. "Come on, Nicole…" he started to say, when she held up a hand.

"No," she said. "No excuses."

"You're human," Flynn said.

"Believe me," she replied, "it will *never* happen again." She knocked his hand away.

"I was just…" he began, when she suddenly froze in place.

"Don't move," she said. "Don't speak."

"Another spider?" Flynn asked, his voice rising a few octaves. "Horribly poisonous multi-legged insect?"

She scanned the jungle around them, then shook her head. "We're surrounded."

Flynn looked around warily. "I don't see anybody," he said.

Suddenly, a swarm of native tribesmen were on all sides of them. Each carried a spear or a primitive bow or a handful of darts.

"Oh," Flynn said. *"Them."*

Nicole nodded. "Them," she agreed.

CHAPTER SEVEN

Traipsing through the jungle at night wasn't the safest plan, but Nicole didn't mind. It was a better than even bet that these natives—whoever they were—would also find the Serpent Brotherhood thugs hot on their heels... and do away with them in some nasty, oh-so-perfect, way. She ducked a branch hanging in their path. Even if they didn't, at the least she and Flynn were getting farther away from them.

Flynn stumbled, almost fell, and she caught him by the arm. "Don't fall down," she said. "They might think you're trying to escape."

"In the *dark?*" he said. "I'd have to be an idiot."

"For all they know, you *are an* idiot."

"Good point," Flynn admitted. "You know, there have been rumors of headhunters operating in this area."

"If they were going to kill us, they'd have done it back at the camp," she told him.

"Oh yeah?" he asked. "What if they wanted to torture us first, and then kill us?"

"That would be different," she said. "Then they'd probably take us back to their village first." Noticing his eyes getting wider, she added, "But this is not the time to panic."

Pointing to a wooden pole decorated with a series of shrunken heads tied to a rope, he said, "Can you think of a *better* time to panic?"

Ignoring the obvious, and trying to keep Flynn focused, Nicole said, "You need to talk to them. What language are they speaking?"

He paused in his rambling panic and said, "I can't quite make out the dialect—they're speaking too fast. It seems to have elements of Kungapakori with a little of the syntax of the Yanomanis and maybe even the Amahuacas."

"The *who?*" Nicole said.

One of the natives leaned forward then and poked her with the point of his spear. Gritting her teeth, she hissed, "Poke me again and I'll break that thing off and stick it up your—"

"She's just kidding," Flynn interrupted. "Kidding." He turned to her. "Piss them off, why don't you? A great idea."

Their trek continued through the dark jungle night. Eventually, they reached the outskirts of a small village. The natives quickly surrounded them—women, children, and men of all ages and sizes—and set up a chorus of jabbering voices. Several minutes later, a big man wearing an elaborate type of headdress stepped out of the throng and began addressing their captors.

Listening, Flynn shook his head ruefully, then stepped forward, feeling far less panicked and far more confident than he had before. He raised his hand and started speaking rapidly, enjoying Nicole's open-mouthed stare of amazement. He loved surprising her.

The Chief grinned, turned to his tribe and said, *"Norte Americanos!"*

Suddenly, the natives were all smiles. They patted Nicole and Flynn in welcome. He turned to her, a bit embarrassed.

"It was just a form of Portuguese," he said. "I was over-thinking it."

It didn't take long at all before the natives had a full-blown celebration going, complete with bonfires, food, drinking and dancing. Flynn and Nicole were seated near the Chief and were treated like visiting royalty.

He leaned over to make himself heard over the noise. "It beats being tortured and strung up as a shrunken head, anyway."

Nicole nodded, watching the five dancers performing in front of them with a combination of interest and wary fear.

A group of native children approached Flynn, chattering away. He smiled and removed several blank pieces of paper from his pack. *"Você gostam de pássaros?"* he asked them. They laughed and nodded yes. He quickly folded the papers into a variety of shapes—a swan, a goose, even a swallow—and gave them to the children.

They laughed with delight and ran off with their new treasures. Flynn looked at Nicole and grinned.

"What did you ask them?" she said.

"I asked them if they liked birds," he replied. "I took a few Origami classes. Kids seem to like it, and I've found that it's a good way to break the ice with them."

She glanced at where the children had settled down to play. "So they do," she said. "You're full of surprises, aren't you?"

The Chief stood up at that moment and gestured grandly at them, making an announcement in a loud voice.

"What's he saying?" she asked him.

"Watch," Flynn told her.

The Chief suddenly began to dance—a wild, crazy series of movements—his arms flapping about his head and around his body, while his feet moved through a complicated series of odd steps.

"The Chief is doing the 'Mongo Dance,'" Flynn explained to her. "I did a Masters thesis once on native mating rituals. This is one of the best. It's a huge honor for us."

Hot, sweaty, and exhausted, the Chief finally stopped. Flynn stood and offered his hand. *"Você honrou-nos extremamente,"* he said. The Chief nodded and wrapped Flynn in a giant hug.

"What did you say to him?" Nicole asked.

"I told him that he had honored us greatly," Flynn explained.

"I'm impressed," she said absently, her head nodding to the music.

Watching her do her best nonchalant act, Flynn smiled. She would be difficult to impress, but there was something about her—not just her beauty, which was stunning—but her toughness combined with her vulnerability that he found almost irresistible. For the first time in his life, he'd met a woman who truly intrigued him.

Impressing her would be worth almost anything.

The celebration lasted into the early morning hours, though it was still dark when the tribe escorted Flynn and Nicole into a private hut and left them to sleep. Looking around, Nicole pointed out the obvious.

"There's only one bed," she said.

"They, uh… seem to think we're a couple," he said, flushing.

"And where did they get that notion, do you suppose?" she asked. Her glare would have melted stone.

"I wouldn't know," he said, trying for a haloed look and failing. "We wouldn't want to offend them."

"Flynn…" she said, a note of warning in her voice.

"I'm sleeping on the floor, aren't I?" he asked.

"Bingo," she said.

As they prepared to rest, Nicole ignored the stern voice of warning in her head and snuck the occasional peak at this new Librarian. He was in better shape than she'd have guessed. Then he noticed her peeking, or she noticed him peeking, and they turned away.

Glancing back once more, she saw that Flynn's gaze was one of sympathy, rather than lust.

"What?" she said. "What is that look for?"

"It's not your fault, you know," he said. "The last Librarian. We're human beings. We can't help who we fall in love with."

She turned away, not wanting to hear his words… or feel his pity.

"You've done an incredible job keeping me alive," he added. "And I know that hasn't been easy."

"I appreciate that," Nicole muttered. "It's my job."

They faced each other, the tension in the room almost palpable.

Suddenly, Flynn lurched into a frenzied imitation of the Mongo Dance, complete with bizarre arm gestures and crazy footwork.

Unable to help herself, Nicole burst out laughing. Perhaps her first real laugh since Edward had been killed. "Please tell me you forgot to take your medication," she said, trying to catch her breath.

"Admit it," Flynn said. "It's getting you a little hot, isn't it?"

"Hot isn't exactly the word I'd use," Nicole said, still laughing.

"These mating rituals may look a little ridiculous," he said, "but these natives really know their stuff." Flynn grabbed his hair and began swinging his head around and around.

Holding her belly, desperate to stop laughing, Nicole laughed until she cried. "That's it!" she said. "Over there! Now!"

Flynn stopped his wild movements. "Oh sure," he said. "Pretend like I'm not getting to you."

"Good night, Flynn," she said, still holding her aching sides. The smile on her face felt funny, like those muscles hadn't really been used in a long while.

Flynn crossed the small hut and laid down on the floor, while Nicole went to the bed, and blew out the small lantern.

"Good night, Nicole," Flynn said. There was a long moment of quiet, and then he added, softly, "Oh yeah. She wants me."

That got her started all over again, and before she knew it, she was laughing again. "Good *night*," she said.

She quickly fell into sleep—the best rest she'd had in many long months.

Nicole opened her eyes, stretched, and turned her head to where Flynn had been sleeping on the floor. *He was gone!*

She leapt to her feet and tore out of the hut, frantic. What if he'd been taken by the Serpent Brotherhood while she slept? He'd be dead, just like Edward, because she'd let her guard down.

She raced through the village, finally stopping a small group of the villagers. "Where's the goofy guy I was with?"

Given her disheveled appearance and panicked stare, combined with the fact that they didn't speak English, the villager only looked at her and shrugged.

"Norte Americano?" Nicole tried again.

They all smiled and nodded, pointing toward the river. Nicole spun around, and spotted Flynn. He was standing near the riverbank with a group of children, all of them laughing. More importantly, all of them *safe*.

She breathed a sigh of relief—which was the precise moment a jeep came barreling through the dense jungle. A native of the region jumped out and scanned the village.

"They're here," he said, his voice carrying in the sudden silence. He pointed toward the village.

"Oh, shit," she said, turning back to the river. "Flynn!" She began running toward him, screaming his name. "Flynn!"

She saw him turn, the smile leaving his face as he spotted the tracker and the other Serpent Brotherhood thugs—including the man and woman from the plane—jumping out of the jeep and preparing to give chase.

Nicole grabbed him by the arm. "Run!" she ordered, pushing him into the dense jungle behind a row of huts. "Don't stop, whatever you do!"

Behind them, the tracker yelled, "There!"

A chorus of shouts went up, "After them!"

"Keep going!" she said. The chase was on for real.

Beside him, Nicole was shoving branches and vines out of their way as they ran through the jungle. He could hear the cultists cutting through the trees behind them.

"Faster," he urged. "Must go faster."

"I *know*," she said, shoving another tangle of vines out of the way.

A small opening in the trees allowed Nicole to surge ahead of him, and she barely slowed as she leapt over a large pit in the ground. He jumped over as well, catching a glimpse of the hole as he passed it. On the other side he suddenly stopped.

"That's an ancient Olmec burial pit!" he said. "*Amazing!*"

Nicole grabbed him by the arm. "You were the one who said faster," she snarled. "You're going to be the one buried in it if you don't keep running."

Flynn nodded, though he dearly wished he could stay to explore the find further. Grabbing a large, leafy branch from a tree, he heaved and broke it loose. Then he laid it over the hole, partially covering the pit.

"Let's go," she said, shoving him forward.

They were barely into the trees on the other side of the clearing when their pursuers burst in behind them.

Flynn listened carefully, heard the leader stop short, trying to warn the others, but it was too late. At least one cultist went in. His screams carried quite clearly in the morning air. He smiled grimly as he ran, then said, "They're still coming."

"I know," she said. "There's another clearing up ahead. Keep going."

But just as she made the clearing, Nicole slammed on the brakes.

They'd reached the edge of a cliff.

The jungle closed in on either side of them. There was nowhere left to run.

Strangely, she chose that moment to turn to him and slap him—hard!—across the cheek. "Don't you ever, *ever* leave my sight again! Do you understand?"

Stung, Flynn said, "Since when did it become 'Slap the Librarian Day'?" He took her arm, then dropped it. "Oh, I get it," he said. "You're just being professional. It's not like you genuinely care for me."

"Shut up!" Nicole said. "God, you… you talk a lot!"

He grinned at her. "I knew you couldn't resist me for long. I have the kind of charm that creeps up on you slowly. Very slowly. Like moss or fungus. It usually takes years." He paused, then added, "And a head injury."

Behind them, the sound of the cultists moving through the jungle was getting closer. They'd be on them any minute.

"You remember yesterday?" Flynn asked. "When you pointed out that whole equation of you being the brawn and I'm the brains?"

"Sure," Nicole said, looking distractedly at the sheer drop in front of them.

He shrugged. "Well, I'm out of ideas. Do you have any?"

Nicole turned to him and smiled. It reminded him of a shark—a hungry shark possessed of an intelligence not usually associated with sea life.

"Why are you smiling?" he asked. "I don't like it when you smile."

"You don't like my smile?" she asked.

"Well, of course," Flynn said, "I *do* like your smile. It's just that it means you're about to do something incredibly dangerous." He thought for a moment, then added, "And that you're going to make *me* do something incredibly dangerous with you."

She reached out and took his hand. "You know me so well."

Then she wrapped her arms around him and jumped off the cliff.

He almost had time to scream.

CHAPTER EIGHT

L ana shoved Rhodes and the tracker out of the way to peer down the cliff and into the raging current of the Amazon River below. The Librarian and his muscle-bound girlfriend surfaced, gasping for air as they were carried away by the river. They were in for a wild ride from the looks of things.

"Did you see that?" she asked Rhodes. "Did you?" She felt a shiver go up her spine. "This Librarian is *incredible.*"

The muscles along Rhodes' jawline locked, and he squeezed the bridge of his nose between his thumb and forefinger. "I don't bloody *believe* it," he snarled. He suddenly pulled his .45 out of the shoulder holster he wore, and pointed it at the local cult members brought along as additional muscle.

"Move," he said, gesturing toward the edge. "You're going."

"¿Qué usted está esperando?" one of them said to the other. Lana quickly translated the question in her mind. He'd asked his fellow what he was waiting for.

"¡No sé nadar!" came the reply.
Lana laughed. The poor chap didn't know how to swim.

"¿Cuál, está usted loco? ¡La caída le matará probablemente!" The words had barely left his mouth when Rhodes shoved them off the cliff. They screamed all the way down.

"What was that last bit?" he asked her.

"Oh, he asked him if he was crazy, since the fall would probably kill him anyway," Lana said. She looked down the cliff, and shrugged. "No need to use the gun on me. I guess I'm next."

"We'll go together," Rhodes said.

They linked arms and jumped.

Nicole surfaced, spit water, and looked for Flynn. The only way to survive this would be to stay together, and the water was churning around them in frothy white and green swirls. Ahead there was a faint roaring sound, which Nicole knew was a waterfall.

"Flynn!" she said.

He popped up nearby, coughing. "We're alive!" he said, smiling. Then he looked down-river, and his face paled.

"Grab onto me," she ordered him. "This is going to get—"

"Roughhhhhhhh!" they both screamed as the waterfall dropped them over the edge.

Somehow, they managed to stay together, and Nicole grabbed Flynn as he surfaced again.

"Grab that branch," she yelled, gesturing wildly.

He almost had it when a surge of water knocked him into her, and they both tumbled back into the current. "Damn it!" she said when she heard the distinctive noise of another falls.

She had barely grabbed him when they went over a second time. This drop was longer and they hit the water hard, the force loosening her grip.

Flynn lifted his head above water, coughing and spluttering. Trying to stay afloat in the raging currents, he spied her and came near. "That wasn't so bad, now was it?" he shouted.

Nicole wrapped her arms around him. "Not half as bad as that's going to be," she said, yelling as yell. The noise in this part of the river was almost deafening.

Ahead of them, another waterfall—gigantic and monstrous—waited. The water surged, pushing them forward.

"This is going to suuuuck!" Flynn yelled as they went sailing over the top of the falls.

This time the fall took longer—enough for it to feel like it was happening in slow motion—and yet Nicole splashed down with incredible force before she'd known the bottom was there. She went under, sucked water, and came back up.

Her eyes scanned for Flynn, saw him, and she furiously swam over to catch onto him again. The current was finally slowing, and she held him while he caught his breath, allowing them to float and drift into calmer water.

When the pace of the river had slowed considerably, Nicole moved them closer to shore. Ahead, the Amazon divided into two tributaries, so this was as good a place to stop as any.

"Which direction now, Einstein?" she asked him.

Suddenly alert, Flynn said, "The book!" and began swimming for shore.

He launched himself out of the water and tore off his backpack. Reaching inside, he removed the ancient text and placed it on a rock, almost sobbing. The book was soaked, the ink smeared in all directions.

"Ruined," he moaned to Nicole as she joined him. "It's ruined."

He closed his eyes, but Nicole knew better. The treasures of the Library were more difficult to destroy than any ordinary book. This one, too, could hold surprises. Yet she felt her jaw sag as the water soaking the pages began to form into individual droplets.

"Flynn, look!" she whispered.

He opened his eyes, and they watched as the water literally slid off the paper and the smeared print returned to normal.

"I don't believe it," he said.

"You'd be surprised how often I've heard that," Nicole said dryly.

"I bet," Flynn said. He turned the page and began to interpret the next clue. "'Follow the sun,'" he read, "'until it ends.'"

"What does that mean?" she asked him.

"It means that we follow the sun until it ends," he grinned. "Sometimes a cigar is just a cigar."

Flynn and Nicole dove back into the Amazon, following the calm waters in this section downstream. Overhead, the jungle grew slowly thicker, the vines heavier and more closely packed together until the growth virtually blocked out the sky overhead. Day had effectively become night.

"I do believe," he said, "that the sun has ended."

"Looks that way," Nicole agreed.

Flynn consulted the book, holding it up so that water wouldn't splash the pages and force him to wait until the magic of the book recreated the text. "We're almost there," he said. "All we have to do now is travel the circumference of the Earth divided by the length of the Fortress of Ollantaytambo."

"How the hell are we going to figure that out?" she asked.

"It's simple, really," he said, pointing. "792 yards this way." He started swimming for the bank, and Nicole followed him to shore.

They climbed out of the water, the humidity so thick and heavy that their wet clothes made virtually no difference to them. "We should check for leeches," Nicole said.

"Leeches?" Flynn asked.

"Yes," she said, smiling. "You wouldn't want one of those in any… sensitive areas, now would you?"

"I think I'll check for myself," Flynn stuttered, imagining all the nooks and crannies on his body a hungry leech might decide to lodge himself. "Of course," he added, "I'd be happy to check you, if you'd like."

"I'll manage, thank you very much," Nicole said.

The slight blush on her cheeks *could* have been from the heat, Flynn thought, but he doubted it.

They took a brief moment to hide behind the foliage and check themselves over for the bloodsuckers. They each found several, but Flynn counted himself fortunate that none of them had chosen extremely sensitive areas on which to latch. Once they were re-dressed, he pointed again the way the needed to go.

This time, he took the lead, while Nicole followed. When they reached the precise spot that, according to the book, they should be, the foliage was so thick and heavy they could only see a few feet in front of them.

Nicole stared at the featureless jungle in front of them. "Nothing," she said. "There's nothing here. You must've gotten something wrong."

Flynn snorted. "I don't get facts wrong," he said. "It's everything else I screw up."

"Well," she said, "let's get to looking, then."

Working at opposite points of a circle, they began pushing aside the foliage, searching for some sign that they were in the right area. Frustrated, Flynn hacked at the vines, tossing pieces over his shoulder and mumbling to himself. Finally, a carved stone was revealed behind one of the walls of vines.

"Ah-ha!" he shouted. He shoved the vines aside, revealing a large, stone doorway. Nicole joined him and within a few minutes, the entrance to an ancient temple was revealed. Presumably, it had been overgrown by the jungle for many, many years, its location a secret unknown to anyone.

"Those markings," Nicole said. "Mayan, aren't they?"

Flynn nodded. "Yes. When the Toltecs invaded Chichen Itza, it was rumored that a group of Mayan priests fled with their entire treasury. The story goes that they built a Mayan temple deep in the Amazon to hide the treasure. They were never heard from again."

Nicole slapped at a buzzing insect. "They were probably eaten alive by mosquitoes," she said. She tapped at the solid stone of the door. "So how do we get inside, genius?"

Flynn moved some of the remaining foliage aside and revealed the handle to the door. "We open it," he said, speaking with exaggerated slowness.

"Funny," she said. "Not funny ha-ha, but funny." She grasped the handle and attempted to move it. The handle wouldn't budge an inch.

She shoved and pulled, and the door remained firmly closed.

Flynn stepped forward to examine the markings on the door. Nicole, apparently misunderstanding his intent, said, "I hardly think your massive physique is going to make a huge difference here."

"You're right," he agreed, ignoring her comment as he continued reading. "These are Mayan numbers. Their priests were obsessed with numbers."

"You would've fit right in," she said.

"You're in a fine mood," Flynn observed. "You must be at your most happy when we're facing almost certain death. These minor annoyances really frustrate the hell out of you, don't they?"

She sighed. "You have no idea."

"Some," he said, grinning at her until she was forced to smile back.

He consulted the book again. "'To get inside,'" he read, "'you must know the time it takes a bird to become a bird again.'" He snapped his fingers. "The Procession!"

"The what?"

"It's the time it takes the constellations—
the Mayans called them 'the Birds of Heaven'—
to make a complete revolution around the sky.
The Mayan priests were the first to discover it."
He stepped up to the door handle. "25, 765 years,
to be precise."

He pressed the corresponding numbers on
the door handle, and gestured. Nicole stepped
forward and pushed on the door. Nothing.

"Got any other bright—" she started to say,
but that was when the ground dropped out from
beneath them.

The sudden fall into darkness was bad. Landing
on solid stone was worse. Nicole landed face
first on a stone, Flynn landed with a heavy thud
next to her. She struggled to her feet.

"Ouch," she said, looking around. "What is
this place?"

Flynn got to his feet. "I'm not sure," he
said.

They were standing on a small stone platform. About a hundred yards away was another

platform of about the same size. On the far side of the room was a door.

Nicole looked down. Below them was a drop of almost a hundred feet that ended in a pit covered with long, wooden spikes. Skeletons of those who had been here before littered the spikes. She mentally corrected herself. Those who had been here just long enough to die.

One of the skeletons was still wearing a fedora; a long whip dangled from the bones of its hand. "You recognize him?" she asked.

Flynn nodded. "I thought that was only a movie thing," he said.

"Someone must have been trying on the role for size," she said. "A bad fit for the part."

Flynn laughed weakly. "This is a Mayan death chamber," he said. "Escape is granted to only those who can solve the secret of the room."

Staring at the bleak scene below, Nicole said, "Then it's a good thing I brought a genius along. How many have solved it?"

"I'd imagine no one has ever made it out alive," he said, gesturing toward the skeletons. "The only way out of this room is the doorway on the other side."

"Okay, *genius,*" she said, stressing the word. "So how do *we* get there?"

"That's the secret," he said.

A deep, grumbling sound came from the darkness behind them, and Nicole turned to see that the wall had started moving—toward them. The platform they were standing on was going to become too small to stand on in a very short period of time.

"That can't be good," she said.

"We'll have to figure out how to make it across before the wall sweeps us into the pit below," Flynn said.

"Really?" she asked. "Any clues in that book of yours?"

"Actually," Flynn said, "no. We're on our own here."

"Perfect," she answered. She rushed to the wall and tried to push against it. Anything that might slow its advance toward them would be helpful, but the wall continued to move inexorably forward.

"What now?" she asked.

"I don't know," Flynn admitted.

Pushing against the wall with all her strength, she gritted her teeth and said, "Now would be a damned good time for you to do something brilliant."

Flynn nodded. "Of course. That's why I'm here."

He was rattled, she saw. "Focus, Flynn! Big mission. Fate of the world."

"I... I..." he stuttered. "Nothing's coming to me, Nicole. I can't think. This has never happened before."

"I knew it!" she yelled. "You're choking, just like I knew you would!"

"Hey!" he said, then paused. "Ahhh, I get it. Reverse psychology. Not bad."

Feeling her feet sliding across the floor, Nicole redoubled her efforts at slowing the wall's advance. No good. "Not reverse psychology," she grated. "Anger! Annoyance!"

The wall was getting closer and closer to pushing them off the edge. Flynn was staring across the room, apparently searching for inspiration.

"Good," he mumbled. "Trying to distract me from the crisis with an implied threat. A sound technique."

"It's *not technique!*" she screamed.

The wall had pushed her back to Flynn's side. There was only a small amount of room left on the platform.

Flynn snapped his fingers. "Got it!" he said. "This chamber is an exact replica of the Great Temple of Teotihaucan: 300 quahuitls by 52 quahuitls. There was a place in the temple where the priests could receive salvation no matter what they did." He pointed. "It would've been right there. Salvation."

"That's mid-air, Sherlock," Nicole said.

"Trust me," he said.

Nicole released her useless grip on the wall and moved to the edge of the platform. "You only live once," she said, staring down into the pit below.

"Unless you believe in Buddhism or Sikhism," Flynn said.

"I hate you so much!" Nicole shouted.

They both jumped at the same time as the wall covered the last inches of the platform. The spikes below looked almost as if they were extending themselves upward when they landed—quite safely—on what appeared to be absolutely nothing at all.

Nicole looked down. It was an invisible stone platform!

"It's an optical illusion," Flynn explained. "The Mayans were nuts about them." He squatted down and tapped on the stone at their feet. "Mirrors," he added. "They were the first tribe in the Americas to use them."

"You could've told me," Nicole said.

"But that wouldn't have been nearly as much fun as the look on your face when we jumped," Flynn said. "Besides, I owed you for that push out of the airplane."

Nicole shook her head and laughed. "Good enough," she said.

"Come on," he said. He began walking confidently toward the platform on the other side of the room. Nicole followed, being certain to step where he stepped. The Mayan illusion was so good that there was no telling where the edge of salvation really was.

They made it safely to the doorway and looked into the room beyond.

From floor to ceiling and wall to wall was a vast treasure horde. A dragon could have happily lazed here in the knowledge that he was the wealthiest of his kind. Urns, ingots, jewels and more were strewn about the room. A king's ransom in gems. The treasury at Fort Knox.

All in one place.

The room glittered with the reflected light. This was the wealth of a nation, Nicole realized, lost in the jungle for hundreds of years.

"It's beautiful," she said.

Flynn stared in awe. "Yes, it is," he breathed.

Before she could caution him, he stepped forward. As his foot came down, Nicole saw the stone beneath it depress downward.

She reached for him, knowing that yet another Mayan trap had just been sprung.

CHAPTER NINE

Flynn felt his weight shift and heard a faint *thwump* behind the walls. In a microsecond, he knew that he'd sprung a trap—and that there was absolutely nothing he could do about it. Then Nicole yanked him backward.

Hundreds of arrows, their tips alight with flame, shot past him, missing him by mere centimeters. They were followed by scores of tiny darts—poisoned, no doubt—that flew from hidden holes in the walls. Beyond those, a giant pendulum swung free, the gleaming blade of a giant axe cutting the air as it passed.

"That was close," he whispered. "*Very* close."

The pendulum stopped.

"What's the saying?" Nicole asked. "'Close only counts in horseshoes, hand grenades and atom bombs'?"

Flynn smiled weakly. "Something like that." He gave her a nod. "Thanks. Again."

"It's what I'm here for," she said. "Shall we go?"

They took one halting step forward, and the cycle started up again: arrows, darts, and axe.

"Apparently," Flynn said, "once it's started, it doesn't stop."

Nicole stared at the passageway closely. "We just need to find the pattern."

They both watched as the various implements of death completed the cycle and then started up again. And again. And once more.

"It's an exact rhythm," Flynn said. "*One,* two, three. *One,* two, three. *One,* two, three." He considered for a moment, then said, "Why is that so familiar?"

"It's called a waltz," she said. "We just have to dance over to the treasure."

"Dance," Flynn said. "Wonderful. Perfect rhythm or we're dead, right?"

"You must've read a book on dancing at some time or another."

"At my high school prom, I crushed the toes of every girl I danced with," he said. "Even my mother wouldn't dance with me."

There was a long pause while Nicole stared at him. "You took your *mother* to your high school prom?"

"I can't believe I just admitted that," Flynn said with a groan. "I didn't exactly take *her*, per se. She was there."

"You took your mother—your *mother*—to your high school prom?"

"She's a very nice lady," he said defensively. "She wanted to go. She even liked the music."

"You have just attained a whole new level of geek status in my eyes," she said. "An Olympian level. Just when I think you might be an almost normal guy, you spring something like this on me."

"Everyone's gotta be good at something," he said.

"Your mother," Nicole repeated.

"Don't start with me," Flynn said. "It was a long time ago. Let's just let it go and concentrate on the passageway dance of death, okay?"

Shaking her head, Nicole said. "Fine. We'll do it together." She wrapped her arms around him, swaying his body back and forth, helping him to get into the rhythm. "It's all in the hips and the butt," she said.

Flynn tried to move with her, but knew he was catastrophically cursed with two left feet. Nicole grabbed him tighter.

"We're going to go now," she whispered in his ear. "Keep to the rhythm."

She swayed with him into the passage, counting. "*One,* two, three…" The flaming arrows shot off the walls, missing them by a hair. "*One,* two, three…"

They continued to waltz, and if it weren't for the certain death sure to befall them, Flynn would have enjoyed being in her arms, her breath in his ear. As it were, he was too busy trying to keep in perfect step to truly enjoy the experience.

The poisoned darts shot out at them. "*One,* two, three…" Nicole whispered, and the darts almost missed them. Flynn felt one tug briefly on his sleeve, but that was it.

"*One,* two, three…" she said, pausing a step as the giant axe pendulum swung in front of them. They danced beneath it, and as it passed back,

Nicole dramatically leaned him back, a graceful dip that allowed him to avoid being decapitated.

"Aren't I supposed to be the one doing the dipping?" Flynn asked. "I'm sure I've read that in a book somewhere, or seen it in a documentary or something."

Nicole grinned. "That was quite exhilarating," she said, stepping into the treasure chamber.

Flynn followed her, watching as she gathered up handfuls of gems and tossed them playfully into the air. The chamber was dazzling. Gemstones the size of ostrich eggs. Golden urns and statues. Ancient coins and jewelry. A king's ransom in wealth.

"There it is," Nicole said. She pointed to a large glass case. Inside was the second piece of the Spear of Destiny. She stepped across the mounds of treasure, reaching for it.

"NO!" Flynn yelled. He grabbed her arm and yanked it away before she could touch the case.

She stared at him, her eyes narrowed. "You'd really better have a damned good reason for doing that."

"These things are always booby-trapped," Flynn answered. "It's in all the movies."

"This *isn't* a movie," she said—but she stepped back and eyed the case warily. "Still."

"Yeah," he said. "Still." He studied the case carefully. "Hmmm…"

Flynn stepped to the other side of the room, pulling Nicole along behind him. He reached down and selected a gigantic diamond from the treasure horde and hefted it a few times in his hand. He heaved it at the case—and missed completely.

"Oh, for the love of…" she said. "Let me do it,"

"I just forgot to factor in the floor's slope," Flynn said. He picked up another huge diamond, and this time his throw was perfect. It crashed into the case, breaking the glass and knocking it over. A split-second later, a huge stone came crashing down from the ceiling, smashing into the spot where they had been standing before.

Nicole stared at the place where she would have died, had it not been for Flynn. She started to say something, stopped, swallowed, tried again, and still came up with nothing.

Flynn patted her on the shoulder and stepped forward, thankful that nothing would be said. Losing her now would be... not good. He truly cared for her, and that was yet another new experience for him on this journey.

The Spear fragment was covered with broken glass, which he gently brushed away. He reached for it, paused, and then grasped it in his hand. He turned and held it up in his fist, lost in the wonder of having recovered at least part of the awesome artifact before the Serpent Brotherhood.

"I... I never thought I could do it," he said. "I mean we."

"I'm just the muscle, Flynn," Nicole said. "Remember?"

"At last count, I'd be dead five times without you."

"Six," she said. "But who's counting?"

"You, apparently," he said.

He looked around the chamber. The Librarian who had hidden the piece here sure had known what he was doing. There was a whole history of very large shoes to fill, but he'd done it so far. For the first time, began to feel that perhaps he could be The Librarian.

"Let's get out of here," he said. "There's another piece yet to be found."

"Lead the way," Nicole said. "And try not to get yourself killed."

Flynn chuckled. "I'll do my best," he said.

"I bet," she muttered.

The path out of the temple was far simpler than the way in had been. Having a working knowledge of Mayan principles of architecture helped, but there were no additional traps or dangers lurking in the walls or the floor to slow them down. After climbing several staircases hewn from stone, Flynn led her to the backside of the door.

"Here we are," he said. "The way out."

"If we have the same luck getting out as we did getting in, we're about to go for a long, dark ride," Nicole said. "Remember?"

"It should open just fine," Flynn said. He shoved at the door and it opened slowly, the rock making a harsh, grating sound. As dim as the area had been before, they still blinked their eyes as they emerged from the temple.

"You understand the ramifications of this?" Flynn was asking, holding up the Spear piece. "If the Spear is real, it brings Biblical history into an entirely new light—"

"Tell you what," she said, interrupting him. "Let's get the last piece, and you and Judson can have a nice, long chat in Aramaic about the history stuff while I take a hot shower—"

She stopped, staring into the clearing. Flynn stumbled into her, and looked ahead to see their pursuers standing a few feet away. All of them were pointing guns at them.

"I believe," the leader said, striding forward, "the phrase is 'Hands up.'"

"Don't move, Flynn," Nicole ordered. She raised her hands.

Flynn did likewise, and the Asian woman stepped forward to take the Spear piece from him. She leaned in, and said, "I just... ah... I really admire your work." Then she winked at him.

Flynn raised an eyebrow, confused. He'd obviously been expecting a beating or torture. A seductive move was about the last thing on his mind.

Nicole said, "So, now what? You kill us both and take the Spear?"

"Not at all," Rhodes said. "We take you to the boss, then *he* gets to kill you." He holstered his gun and jerked a thumb at them. "Bring them!" he snapped at his men.

Flynn stumbled over a root protruding from the ground. Nicole caught him before he fell.

"Don't make any sudden moves," she said. "Not even by accident. They might think you're trying to run for it and shoot you for your trouble."

"Sorry," he mumbled. "Tripped."

"I know," she said. "Just be careful. This isn't the time for mistakes."

He nodded in agreement. Ahead, the man and several cultists were leading them back through the dense jungle foliage. Behind, the woman and the rest of the Serpent Brotherhood were ensuring that they didn't escape. Though she seemed willing enough to harm him, she'd also acted almost... girlish, like she was flirting with him back at the temple.

"Hey," he said, catching her attention. "How much farther is it...?"

"Lana," she replied. "Why? You in a hurry to die, big boy?"

He shook his head. "Hardly. But it's been kind of a long day, you know."

"You'll get to rest soon enough," she replied. "The camp is just ahead."

Flynn turned his attention back to the path and trying to figure out a way to escape. Nothing really came to him—they were surrounded, and now the Serpent Brotherhood had *two* of the three pieces needed to assemble the Spear of Destiny. Some Librarian *he'd* turned out to be.

After a trek of several miles, the density of the vines thinned and Flynn could see a clearing ahead.

"That's a relief," he said to Nicole, pointing. "My feet are killing me."

"If that's your only worry, you're a braver man than I thought," she said. "We'll be damn lucky if only our feet are killing us."

The clearing opened before them, and a small campsite, complete with tents and a fire, was already in place. Sitting in a chair was the tracker who'd been leading them through the jungle.

Lana stepped over to him and handed over a wad of bills. The tracker nodded once in appreciation, slipped the money into a pocket, and walked out of the campsite. His work here was done. As he left, fading into the jungle like a ghost, he passed a tent that was slightly larger than the others.

The flap opened, and a man stepped out. Even in the shadows, Flynn could see the tell-tale serpent tattoo, running up the man's forearm and over the back of his hand. His face was hidden in the dim light. Lana walked over and handed him the Spear piece and Flynn's backpack.

"I knew you'd bring me the piece, Nicole," he said.

"Edward?" Nicole gasped. Her voice was a hollow whisper.

It was Edward Wilde! Flynn felt his eyes widen in shock.

"Wait a minute!" he said. "You're the last Librarian. You're supposed to be dead."

"And yet here I stand," Wilde said.

"I saw you die," Nicole said. "I... I saw them kill you."

"You saw a very elaborate series of special effects," countered Wilde. "Your tears were a perfect touch. I couldn't have planned it any better myself."

"Then they really didn't cut off your head?" Flynn asked.

Wilde looked him over and scowled. "And *you're* the new Librarian? Not very quick on the uptake, are you?"

"But why, Edward?" Nicole asked. "Why?"

"Absolute power," he answered. "It's the ultimate aphrodisiac." He looked her over appreciatively. "And you know how I love a good aphrodisiac."

"You bastard!" Nicole screamed. She ripped free from the cultists surrounding her. "I'll kill you myself!" She leapt forward, grabbing Wilde by the throat.

Several of the thugs tried to pry her off him, but Nicole was too strong and too fast by a huge margin—that, and she was really, *really* pissed off, Flynn thought. Finally, Wilde managed to take a step back and he slammed a fist into her jaw, knocking her to the ground. Stunned, Nicole didn't rise.

He pulled a nasty-looking gun from a holster, stood over her, calmly cocked it, and pointed it at her head. "Goodbye, Nicole," he said. "It was really nice to see you again."

Suddenly realizing that he was about to lose the one woman he's ever truly cared about, Flynn jumped forward, putting himself between Wilde and Nicole. "You can't kill her," he said.

"And why not?" Wilde asked. "She's served her purpose. She wiggled her cute little ass to inspire you to get me—" he held up the Spear piece in his other hand "—this."

"You'll never find the last piece without me," Flynn said. "And I won't do it without her."

"I don't need you," he said, grinning. "I have…" He reached into Flynn's backpack and pulled out the ancient book of clues. The grin on the man's face rapidly faded as he stared at the strange hieroglyphics.

Flynn smiled, knowing what Wilde was about to find.

"The Language of the Birds?! Nobody can read this!" Wilde said.

"Nobody," Nicole said, rising to her feet, "except a *real* Librarian." She brushed her hands against her pants. "We should've suspected you all along—you were charming enough, but didn't have the real intellect for the job."

"Don't push me, Nicole," Wilde snarled. "I can find ways to make him cooperate."

"Tgggsaxhu axhjai uahg pbbsy cygywj gvva ahioqjq," Flynn said. "In the Language of the Birds, that means you're up a creek, and I have the only paddle."

Wilde raised his gun again, pointing it at Nicole. "Tell me where the third piece is and I'll let her live."

"Don't tell him!" she said.

Flynn shrugged. "It's in Shangri-La."

Wilde shoved the gun into Nicole's temple. "Don't screw with me," he said. "That's a legend."

Flynn forced a casual laugh. Wilde didn't seem completely sane—or at least he didn't seem like a man who thought things through. This wouldn't be the time to make him really angry—it could get Nicole killed.

"You, of all people," he said, "should know that many of the so-called legends are true.

Shangri-La is at the top of Mount Kailash in the Himalayas."

"Idiot," Nicole muttered under her breath.

"Well, excuse *me* for trying to save your life," Flynn said.

"My life isn't as important as protecting the Spear," Nicole said. "Why do I have to keep telling you that?"

"I must be a slow learner," he replied. "Of course, he won't get anywhere near it unless I'm there to interpret the clues in the book." He looked pointedly at Wilde. "And if you kill her, you may as well kill me. I won't tell you anything else, and you'll get to spend the winter months wandering around Mount Kailash looking for a place you will *not* be able to find without me."

Wilde laughed and re-holstered his gun. "I should've listened to Lana instead of Rhodes about you, Flynn," he said. "You're more clever than you appear."

"It's the hair," Flynn said. "Something about the style that makes people think I'm a nerd."

"It's *something*," Nicole muttered.

"So, we're at an impasse," Wilde said. "Fair enough." He turned to the rest of his thugs. "Break camp," he ordered. "We're going on a little trip together."

Flynn exhaled in relief. At the least, he'd bought Nicole some time to figure out how they were going to escape.

Wilde gestured at Lana and Rhodes. "You two keep a sharp eye on them," he said. "No mistakes."

"It will be my pleasure," Lana purred, stepping forward to within inches of Flynn.

"Perfect," Nicole said, her voice harsh and sarcastic. "It'll be just like old times."

CHAPTER TEN

N icole watched her former lover—and the last Librarian—Edward Wilde out of the corner of her eye. The trek back through the Amazon jungle had taken considerably less time with the full resources of the Serpent Brotherhood at his disposal. Heavy-duty jeeps and a score of people to cut down or move obstacles had made the journey to San Paolo almost pleasant compared to how she and Flynn had gotten to the temple with the lost fragment of the Spear.

On the other hand, they were now both captives, and Flynn was determined to help Edward in order to protect her. Several times, they'd had whispered conversations about escaping, only to decide that the timing wasn't right and the chances were less than optimal. "About the same as Satan setting up a raspberry snow cone stand in South Hell," was how she'd put it to him. Flynn had agreed, and it wasn't long after that they'd arrived in San Paolo.

They spent one night there—at a posh hotel under heavy guard—which had at least given them the opportunity to get cleaned up and into a new set of clothes. Flynn's were ragged and torn, and hers weren't in much better shape. Edward had provided the clothing and a lavish meal, and the next morning found them at the airport, boarding a private jet and heading for the Himalayas.

After a long flight, and another night in a decadent hotel, they were driven to a nearby airstrip, where they climbed aboard a large helicopter. Edward had always had a taste for luxury—the best foods and wines, the nicest hotels, the fanciest clothing. He was a man who enjoyed the finer things in life and reveled in the pleasure they brought him: if it was a woman he wanted, he dominated her senses with attention; if it was an object they were trying to retrieve, every aspect of the mission would be done as comfortably as possible; and if it had to do with money or power, Nicole admitted to herself, then he was absolutely fascinated. She should have seen it coming, his conversion to the Serpent Brotherhood—they'd offered him everything he truly valued in life: wealth, comfort and power. She loved him once, and now, given half a chance, she'd kill him herself.

The chopper banked over a glorious range of mountains. The clean, white snow sparkled with orange and yellow reflections as the sun rose and cast its light on the crags. She and Flynn were hog-tied and sitting next to each other on the floor, while Edward directed the pilot based on Flynn's information.

"You know," Flynn said, interrupting her thoughts, "at least you didn't fail in your job. He's still alive."

Gritting her teeth, knowing that he was trying to make her feel better, Nicole took a long time turning her stare from Edward to Flynn. Her cold gaze actually caused Flynn to flinch a little.

"You are *so right*," she said. "He just faked his own death and became the head of the very evil organization we'd been fighting together for years. That's *so* much better."

Edward leaned out of his seat, shoving the ancient book in front of Flynn's face. "That's Mount Kailash," he said, pointing to a spectacular peak visible out of the window. "Where's your Shangri-La?"

"We can't find it from the air," Flynn said. "All the clues are on the ground."

Edward nodded once and turned to the pilot. "Find a place to put us down," he ordered.

The pilot banked the chopper and headed for a snow-covered clearing.

Good, Nicole thought. *On the ground, I'll have a much better chance of killing Edward and getting us out of here.*

As he climbed out of the chopper, Rhodes shoved Flynn forward and he nearly fell face-first into the snow. "Move it," he ordered. "The day's not getting any longer."

Flynn caught himself and continued on. Next to him, Nicole kept her silence, watching as Wilde's cultists gathered mountain-climbing gear and arrayed themselves in a line guaranteed to prevent escape.

Wilde took a deep breath of the crisp air and grinned. "Beautiful," he said.

"What do you want me to do, sir?" the chopper pilot asked.

"We're going to have to climb up," Wilde said. "But stay ready to fly up and meet us."

"Yes, sir," the pilot answered, then clambered back into his seat.

"All right, Carson," he said. "Which way?"

Flynn indicated a very narrow, rocky path. "That way," he said. "And tell Rhodes here to stop shoving me around. You wouldn't want me to slip off this mountain and have a fatal accident before you found the last piece."

"No," Wilde said, "I wouldn't." He turned to Rhodes. "Keep your hands to yourself," he snapped. "We need him a while longer yet."

"But he won't shut up!" Rhodes said. "He's constantly asking questions and babbling on like an old woman!"

"I don't care if he asks you a million questions all the way up the side of this mountain!"

Wilde roared. "I don't pay you to think—I pay you to do as you're told. And you've been told to keep your damn hands off him. Got it?"

Rhodes nodded, then stalked off, muttering under his breath.

"You two take point," Wilde said, motioning for Flynn and Nicole to lead the group up the path. "That way, we can keep an eye on both of you." He made a vague gesture with his hands. "And besides, Nicole *does* present a nice addition to the view."

She didn't reply, just headed in the direction Flynn had pointed out. He trailed along behind her.

The path was ice-covered and rocky, making each step a potentially fatal fall or a broken ankle. Several times, Flynn and Nicole steadied each other. One series of switchbacks led to another, the route becoming steeper and more dangerous as they climbed. Eventually, they passed through the first cloud layer and came to a branching in the path.

Flynn stopped and pulled out the book from his backpack. "Give me a moment," he said, studying it.

"It's too damn cold to stop moving for long," Nicole warned him.

"Don't I know it," he said without looking up from the text. "I think I liked the Amazon better."

"I think it's exhilarating," Wilde said, coming up from behind. "But she's right. Which way now?"

Flynn snapped the book closed. "This way," he said, pointing. He put the book back in his pack and continued on.

Beside him, Nicole was practically stalking up the mountain. Flynn could feel the energy in her—coiled and waiting for the right moment to spring. He didn't want to be responsible for her death, or for leading Wilde to the final fragment.

"Listen," he said to her, keeping his voice soft. "I'm leading them right to it. Nicole, I want to thank you for everything you've done for me. And whatever happens, it's not your fault." He kept his gaze locked with hers a moment longer, then reached down and unclipped his safety harness.

A single half-step, and he was over the edge and falling.

Flynn closed his eyes. It would be good, he thought, to have at least stopped the Serpent Brotherhood from complete success.

Suddenly, a line snagged around his wrist, nearly wrenching his shoulder out of its socket. He looked up, and his eyes locked with Nicole's. She'd snared him with her own safety line, his feet dangling over the edge of the precipice. He'd only dropped a couple of feet.

She yanked on the line, using her strength to drag him back up. "Not on my watch," she snarled.

"My life isn't as important as the Spear," he said, still on his knees.

"Yes, it is," she said. "You're The Librarian." She reached out a hand and helped him up. "I didn't think you had the guts for that, but I won't underestimate you again, Flynn." She re-attached the line to his harness, ensuring his safety once again.

Wilde strode forward and hooked Flynn to his own rope, and shoved him forward. "You're leading me on a wild goose chase," he said. "I should save you the trouble and kill you myself."

He pulled his gun out and pointed it at Flynn.

Flynn began backing up, keeping his hands raised. Behind him, the face of the mountain slowly opened into a deep chasm—from the air it would have been invisible. Wilde closed in, insane emotions chasing each other across his face, when he froze in his tracks. His jaw dropped open, and his eyes widened. For a split-second, Flynn wondered what could be behind him that was so scary it would stop even a mad-man like Wilde.

He turned around, and the vista that opened before him literally took his breath away. A beautiful valley, green even in the winter, filled the bottom of the chasm. He walked forward and the others silently followed as the legendary paradise was revealed to them in all its glory.

The rays of the sun crept over the rim, bathing the valley in a golden light. In the distance, intricate, hand-carved pagodas offered places to pause and take in the scenery. Gardens of flowers and other plants were carefully arrayed in a visually stunning presentation, by which colors of every hue could bedazzle the eye. As the sun followed them in, a rainbow appeared over the valley, adding another dimension to an already breathtaking vista.

At the center of the valley, a domed palace was the jewel—white marble with filigreed patterns of gold and red, minarets with silken flags. Yet for the opulence and beauty here, there was also a profound sense of peace. Ahead of them, several men dressed in monk robes left the front entrance of the palace and came forward.

"It's real," Wilde whispered. "True paradise."

"Of course it's real," Flynn said. "But it's still wonderful to see."

The monks reached them, and the eldest one stepped forward, his head bowing in greeting. "Welcome," he said. "It's long been prophesied that you would come today."

The cultists all pulled out their guns, pointing them at the monks. The metallic sound of slides falling into place filled the valley.

"We want the Spear piece," Wilde said. "Now."

Following the monks toward the palace, Flynn marveled at the nuances of the architecture. A thousand tiny details had gone into the beauty of the building, as well as the grounds around it.

"Excuse me," he said to the monk who appeared to be the leader. "How long did it take to do all this? How long has it existed?"

The older man smiled. "Many years," he said. "Over a thousand." He bowed, and added. "Paradise is possible, but it takes great patience and care to create it."

"I suppose so," Flynn said.

Behind him, he heard Rhodes mutter, "See? Question after question."

No one bothered to offer a reply, and Flynn continued to marvel at the sights while Wilde's thugs kept their guns trained on the monks. They made their way inside, and into an interior courtyard. On the back wall was a large statue of Buddha, sculpted with great care and detail from solid gold. The leader of the monks gestured toward it.

"The Spear fragment you seek is hidden inside," he said.

Wilde gestured with his gun. "Open it," he said.

The old monk shook his head. "We cannot. We are merely the Keepers. We have no idea how to open it."

"Fortunately," Wilde said, "*he* does." He jerked a thumb at Flynn, then shoved him forward. With his free hand, he grabbed Nicole by the arm and dragged her with him. The three of them moved up a set of stairs that led to the statue.

Flynn studied it carefully. Carved around the Buddha's exposed navel—which was an emerald the size of an ostrich egg—were a series of hieroglyphics written in the Language of the Birds.

"Get the Spear piece," Wilde said, yanking Nicole closer, "or I'm blowing her brains out." He pointed his gun at Nicole's temple.

Trying to remain calm, Flynn removed the ancient book from his pack and opened it, reading for the last needed clue. As he reviewed the passage, he shook his head in dismay. "This can't be right," he muttered.

"What?" Wilde said.

Tracing a finger along the ancient writing, he said, "It can only be opened with the name of God."

"Hurry up," Wilde snapped.

"Hel-lo?" Flynn said, unable to keep the annoyance out of his voice. "Anybody home? Umm... the name of God is just the biggest secret ever. In four thousand years, nobody's been able to figure it out, and you expect me to come up with it in a matter of seconds?"

Wilde pressed the barrel of his gun into Nicole's temple, twisting it harder. "Just do it, *Librarian.*"

Flynn thought rapidly. There were some riddles and questions to which the best answers were guesses. He broke into a large grin. Why not? he thought. It's as good an answer as any.

He reached out and pressed two letters on the statue. "M.E.," he said. "Me."

The Buddha's belly began to open, slowly revealing a hidden cache inside.

"How about that?" Flynn asked, still grinning. "It worked."

"You were *guessing?*" Wilde asked in a strangled voice.

"God is within us all," Flynn said. "Is he not?"

Inside the Buddha, the third and final piece

of the Spear was visible. The blade portion, gleaming in the dim light, had only to be lifted from within, and it would be done.

Flynn gestured. "There it is," he said. "Take it."

Wilde reached forward to grab the piece, then suddenly stopped, snatching his hand back. A dark smirk lit his face. "No," he said. "I think not. You take it."

Flynn gulped. There was bound to be a trap here—perhaps several. He slowly reached into the belly, his hands shaking. He wrapped his right hand around the piece, and that was when he saw the pressure plate beneath it. He'd have to move quickly and with great care—this was their last chance to stop Wilde and the Serpent Brotherhood from obtaining all three pieces of the Spear.

"Problem?" Wilde asked.

"No…" Flynn said. As he gingerly withdrew the Spear piece from the Buddha's belly, he did a little head-fake, looking at Wilde, then back to the fragment, while pressing the trap mechanism with his other hand.

He winced, preparing for the worst.

Nothing happened.

Wilde grabbed the Spear piece from his hand, then pulled a radio from his belt. "Lock onto my signal," he ordered the chopper pilot. "Fly up here—now."

Suddenly, the Buddha began to sink into the floor. The palace rocked as a violent shock wave rolled through it.

"It's about time," Flynn muttered. "The one time I actually *want* the trap to work…"

The monks moved without warning, launching themselves at Wilde's minions in a frenzy of kicks and punches that would have made Jet Li jealous.

Wilde leapt down the steps, clutching the piece to his chest. Nicole lunged after him, and kicked his feet out from beneath him. He tumbled down the last few steps, and Nicole triumphantly lifted the Spear piece he'd dropped as he fell.

Beyond them, the monks were tearing through the Serpent Brotherhood thugs like a team of crazed, scythe-wielding farmers through a cornfield. Even the older monk was whirling about the room, felling thugs with sharp, rapid blows from his fists, his robes billowing around him like a cloud.

Two of the cultists broke free from the fray and jumped at Flynn. He ducked, spun, and punched each of them in the solar plexus, mimicking a move he'd seen Nicole do. As they doubled over, he slammed their heads on the Buddha's belly. They collapsed in a heap.

"Not bad," Nicole said. "Not bad at all. You might live through this yet." She jumped down the steps, fighting her way through the crowd.

Flynn smiled proudly and moved to follow her, when he saw Rhodes come charging at him, death in his eyes.

The man had every intention of killing him, and somehow Flynn just knew that he wouldn't be nearly as easy to dispatch as the others had been.

CHAPTER ELEVEN

Nicole saw Rhodes go rushing past her, and spun to go after him. This man would be out of Flynn's league—even his new and improved one. Rhodes leapt into the air, slamming a booted foot into The Librarian's face, then spinning around and jumping onto Flynn from behind.

More out of sheer instinct than any plan, Flynn leaned forward, flipping Rhodes over his head and tossing him onto the stone steps. At that moment, a huge chunk of the ceiling collapsed, smashing into the floor between them. Nicole grabbed Flynn before he could get any seriously macho ideas in his head, and dragged him away.

"Let's go," she said. "We can relive it later—if we survive."

They'd almost reached the exit when Wilde appeared out of the chaos. He jumped in front of them, his pistol pointed at them. "I want that third piece, Nicole."

"A man in hell wants ice water," she said. "That doesn't mean he's going to get it."

Behind them, the temple began to collapse in on itself. With the speed of a striking cobra, Nicole whirled and threw the Spear fragment back into the temple.

Wilde's eyes went wide. "NO!" he shouted, and ran after it.

Nicole grabbed Flynn's arm. "We're out of here," she ordered. "Right now." She dragged him outside before he could protest, the monks hot on their heels as the entire structure of the beautiful palace shuddered.

In the room, Wilde screamed, "Find the piece!" He and his thugs dodged falling chunks of the ceiling in a desperate search for the Spear.

"Keep going," Nicole said to Flynn.

"Where?" Flynn asked.

"There!" she said, pointing to where the helicopter was landing in the distance. "Come on!" She began running for it, knowing that Flynn would follow.

They raced across the valley, glancing back from time to time at the chaos of the crumbling paradise behind them. The reached the chopper, and Nicole leapt inside, driving a viscous elbow into the pilot's temple, and knocking him out cold.

She flung him out of his seat, and followed to land lightly on the ground. Flynn caught up and she yelled, "Get in!"

"What if they get the Spear piece?" Flynn said.

Nicole grinned and reached down, pulling the final section from the sheath on her leg.

"If you want to hide something…" she said.

"Do it in plain sight," they finished together.

The old monk who had led them into the palace came running toward them. Other than a dark smudge on one shoulder of his robe, he appeared none the worse for the wear. The fight and the temple collapse didn't even have him breathing hard.

"Guard it well," he told them. "The Spear can open doors that are best kept closed."

"What about all this?" Flynn said, gesturing at the destruction around them.

"Be at peace, my friend," the old monk said. "Paradise, much like many of the relics you protect, is not so easily destroyed. Shangri-La will be healed."

Flynn nodded, and followed Nicole into the chopper. At that moment, Rhodes and Lana stumbled out of the crumbling temple.

"There!" Lana shouted.

Rhodes pulled his gun and began firing, the whine of bullets splitting the air. Flynn and Nicole ducked as several pierced the roof.

Nicole grabbed the downed pilot's gun and returned fire through the open door. "Flynn, you've got to fly it!"

Staring at the controls, Flynn muttered, "No problem. Just 'fly' a helicopter. I do that kind of thing everyday."

"Now, Flynn!" she ordered. Right now, the distance and angle were making it equally hard for Rhodes and Lana to shoot accurately, but they were closing the gap as they advanced.

"Main principles," he said, "are lift and thrust… easy as pie."

Flynn grasped the controls, and Nicole turned her attention back to Rhodes and Lana. She aimed and fired at the running targets, missing, but the barrage kept them on the dodge rather than running straight at them.

The whirring of the rotors sped up, and the chopper began to lift. The only problem was that Flynn was apparently having trouble controlling it—the helicopter swerved violently from side to side, wobbling like a poorly wound toy.

Nicole leaned back away from the door, still shooting at Lana and Rhodes, keeping them down.

The chopper swayed again, and Flynn cursed. "Horrible high-velocity pie of death!"

The chopper zigzagged across the valley floor, tossing Nicole around like a ragdoll. "Damn it," she swore, finally buckling herself into her seat.

Flynn fought the helicopter like it was a living thing, while bullets whined through the air like deadly, angry bees.

"Get us in the air, Flynn!" Nicole said, ducking as another barrage of shots whipped through the roof.

"I think I've got it now," he said, sounding triumphant as the chopper finally lifted up and away.

Below, the temple completed its collapse, and Rhodes and Lana stopped firing. Even at this distance, Nicole could see the anger and frustration etched on their faces.

Flynn banked the chopper, sweeping up the mountain face in a smooth, steep ascent that took it over the rim of the chasm and the tops of the mountains beyond.

They were both silent for a moment, marveling at the view and the fact that somehow they were both still alive *and* had the Spear fragment. Nicole looked over at Flynn, noting the changes in him, the way that the nerd was being slowly replaced by a more confident man.

After a long moment of silence, she said, "I've seen worse."

Flynn looked at her, and they both began to laugh.

Mongolia was famous for many things, histori-
cally speaking, but Flynn realized that it was
never going to be known for its hotels. The
place they'd found might be described as
"quaint" in generous terms, but compared to the
last places they'd stayed, it was just a dump. But
it was, at least for now, a safe place to take a
much-needed rest before heading back to the
United States with the Spear piece and formu-
lating a plan for getting the other two back.

   After finding a place to stash the chopper,
they'd walked several miles before reaching the
outskirts of this small city and finding a pedi-
cab to take them to a hotel. Flynn used his
knowledge of languages to negotiate for a
room, and now he paced back and forth in front
of an old, black and white television, waiting for
Nicole to get done with her turn in the rickety
shower. He felt a strange, nervous energy that
he hadn't expected—he should have been bone-
tired.

   Suddenly, the television flickered to life,
and Judson appeared on the screen.

   "Mr. Carson," he said.

Flynn did a quick double-take, but surprises were not as frequent for him as they'd been at the beginning of his adventure.

"Everybody in the Library can rest easy," he said. "We definitely have the third Spear piece. It's right…" He scanned the room, looking for it.

It wasn't there! He began tossing the threadbare blankets aside, desperate sweat breaking out on his brow. Finally, he peered under the bed.

"…here," he finished lamely. "Absolutely safe." He quickly filled Judson in on the events that had occurred since he'd left New York, including the discovery that Edward Wilde, once *the* Librarian was now the head of the Serpent Brotherhood.

"Good work, Flynn," Judson said. He thought for a minute, then added. "I still can't get over the fact that Wilde joined the Serpent Brotherhood. He was a fine Librarian. It's a good thing we have a better one now."

Flynn smiled, pleased at the compliment. A knock sounded at the door. "Hold on a moment, Judson," he said. He turned to answer the door, glanced back and saw that Judson was gone. "Someday, he's going to have to tell me how he does that."

He answered the door to find a bellhop wearing a mismatched uniform. He was carrying a pair of wine flutes and an ice bucket with a bottle of champagne in it.

"I didn't order any champagne," Flynn said.

"I did," a soft voice said behind him. Both Flynn and the champagne-bearing bellhop looked toward the bathroom.

Nicole, her hair still wet, stood in the doorway in a short bathrobe—short enough to display long, tan, muscular legs. She adjusted the belt around her waist, allowing just a hint of the even more sensuous beauty beneath the terrycloth.

The ambient temperature in the room rose up by a solid twenty-five degrees—at least that's how it felt to Flynn. His face flushed, and sweat broke out in beads on his forehead.

Nicole walked gracefully across the room and took the champagne from the bellhop. "Thank you," she said, then shut the door. She then took the two glasses, popped the cork on the bottle, and poured.

Flynn stared openly, unable to get over how her tough girl image seemed in complete contradiction to this beautiful, sexy woman standing in his hotel room in a skimpy bathrobe, pouring champagne. Well, tough and sexy wasn't such a bad combination...

He took the offered glass of bubbly, and raised it in a silent toast. Nicole smiled and said, "To success—even on a limited basis."

Flynn laughed. "To still being alive."

They both drank deeply.

Nicole leaned against the dresser, sipping her champagne. "You know, you're not the incredible pansy I thought you were." She paused for a moment, then added, "Of course, *no one* could actually be the incredible pansy I originally thought you were."

"Thanks," he said. "And you're not the raving psychopath I thought you were."

She raised a delicate eyebrow.

"Well, actually," he said, "you are. But in a good way."

She smiled, took a smooth step forward, and Flynn felt his throat almost close around a desperate gulp of air.

"What's wrong?" Nicole asked, slowly closing the distance between them.

"You're smiling," he said softly.

"I know," she said, then wrapped her arms around him and kissed him.

Her lips were soft, her skin still damp from the shower. Flynn had thought of kissing her, had wondered what it would be like to have her in his arms, and now he knew. It was Shangri-La in human female form. She melded against him, her tongue delicately exploring his mouth, and he responded in kind.

She leaned back slightly, not leaving his embrace, and said, "You must've read a book or two on how to make love." It was a half-statement, half-question.

Flynn reddened in embarrassment. "Hundreds, actually," he admitted.

"Good," she said, then kissed him again.

Lost in the moment, the first few rings of his cell phone didn't even faze him. Finally, the harsh sound penetrated his mind, but Nicole reached for it first. She clicked the button to answer it and said, "Flynn's busy. He can't talk." Then she tossed the phone on the dresser and turned her attention back to kissing him.

Vaguely, before he was totally lost in her heated embrace, Flynn thought he heard his mother's voice from thousands of miles away yell, "A woman answered my son's cell phone!" A chorus of women's voices responded and then his mother added a resounding, "Yes!" before the line went silent.

He agreed completely.

Flynn cracked open one eye, letting the light from the dirty window penetrate only enough for him to assess the room. His clothes were strewn everywhere, and Nicole's robe was in a heap on the floor. He raised himself up on one elbow.

It really had happened. Grinning happily, he turned to where Nicole was no doubt sleeping...

And realized she was gone.

Perhaps she'd gone for some coffee or breakfast. He thought about it. Her silent, sudden passion.

Then it hit him. He slid over and leaned down, looking under the bed. Flynn felt the blood drain from his face.

The Spear piece was gone!

Flynn leapt out of bed and hurriedly wrapped the sheet around his body. Throwing open the door, he ran down the hallway and down the steps to the lobby, looking no doubt, like a crazy man.

Using his limited knowledge of Mongolian, he asked the people in the lobby, "Has anybody seen the incredibly beautiful woman I was with?"

The hotel employees shook their heads, their looks ranging from shock to humor.

"What's the matter? You've never seen a naked guy wrapped in a sheet before?"

The lobby television flickered to life, and Flynn turned toward it, realizing that Judson would be there. "Is there a problem, Flynn?" he asked.

"Nicole and the Spear are gone!" he said. "They may have taken her or…" His voice trailed off as the possible alternatives ran through his mind.

"Or?" Judson prompted.

"Or she's been in cahoots with Wilde and the Serpent Brotherhood all along!" Flynn groaned. "Cahoots! We've been cahooted!"

"Calm down," Judson said. "It's not all lost. It took great power to sunder the Spear into three pieces. It will take even more to fuse those pieces back together again."

"How much?" Flynn asked.

Judson appeared lost in thought for a moment, then said, "Well, strip all the mysticism silliness aside, and you'd need a localized electromagnetic field registering over fifteen on the Schumm scale."

Flynn paced back and forth in the hotel lobby, thinking. "Fifteen on the Schumm scale! That's... The only place where that kind of energy's ever been registered was during a peak full moon at the Great Pyramid when it had its capstone— which it no longer has. The Egyptian government refuses to replace it..."

Suddenly, the memory of his last work at the University cascaded through his mind like an ocean wave. The detailed reconstruction of the Great Pyramid—complete with its capstone. It was a scale model, but it could very well work.

He snapped his fingers. "The next peak full moon is—" he calculated quickly in his head "—tomorrow night."

Judson nodded in agreement.

"Call the Marines, Judson," Flynn said. "I'm coming home."

Judson nodded once, and the screen went blank. As Flynn turned to leave, he noticed that all the hotel employees were staring at him as though he'd lost his mind.

"Let me guess," he said. "I take it you don't see anybody on the television?"

They shook their heads.

"Of course you don't," Flynn muttered. He turned and dashed out the front door, which slammed shut behind him.

A second later, he ran back in the door. "Clothes. Need the clothes," he muttered, heading back to his room.

Flynn leaned back in his seat in the first class section of the plane. Wilde may have been a crazy man, but he did know how to travel in comfort, and given the length of the flight and what Flynn had endured to get here, the extra expense—billed to the Library's international account—felt like a deserved reward. Still, the plane couldn't move fast enough for him.

The sooner he got back to New York, the sooner this could be settled, once and for all.

He glanced around the cabin again, taking careful stock of the passengers. Not a serpent tattoo in sight.

Flynn sighed and signaled the stewardess for a beverage.

At least this time, he reflected, *I don't have to learn an ancient language in a few hours, or jump from the plane without a parachute.*

With any luck at all, it would be a quiet, uneventful flight.

What he would need to do when he got home, however, would be anything but quiet and uneventful.

Edward Wilde would have to be stopped.

And if Nicole really was a traitor... she'd have to be stopped as well.

Flynn grimaced. Some trips offered more to look forward to than others.

CHAPTER TWELVE

The full moon hanging over the New York City skyline was huge—a pale white orb that lit the night sky in a ghostly luminescence. Flynn crossed the street, a fleeting shadow, and headed for the entrance to the university museum. There was no one around, and a sign on the door read RADON LEAK: CLOSED UNTIL THURSDAY in big block letters.

He grasped the door handles and tried to force them open. No luck.

A faint whistle from a nearby row of bushes caught his attention. Curious, he walked over to find Judson crouched down, examining a map of the museum's infrastructure.

"The museum's ventilation system can be accessed from here," he said. "Oh, and welcome home."

"Where are the Marines?" Flynn quipped.

Judson pulled up a shirtsleeve and revealed a tattoo of the Marine insignia. *"Semper fi,"* he said.

"Great," Flynn said softly. "You're a Marine. Wonderful."

"I just want you to know, Flynn, that you've already exceeded my expectations. I'm very proud of you." Judson laid a hand on Flynn's shoulder. "Now, let's go get that Spear back."

Flynn swallowed and followed Judson into the dark shadows on the side of the building, and from there, into a ventilation access duct. It was a tight fit for two men, but they managed to squeeze inside and wiggle through, snake-like, on their bellies.

"You know," Flynn whispered after snagging his shirt and scrapping his arm on a piece of aluminum, "a lot of this wasn't in the original job description."

Judson chuckled. "I know. But most job descriptions are more like… rough outlines. Think of it as a sketch, rather than the full glory of a painting."

"Oh, it's been glorious," he said sarcastically.

Judson stopped and turned his head enough to make eye contact. "But it has been, hasn't it?" he asked.

Flynn thought for a second, then nodded. "Most fun I've ever had in my life."

"I thought so," Judson said.

They continued to crawl along the shaft until they found an opening large enough to let them inside the building itself. From there, Flynn was able to take the lead, and he headed for a balcony that he knew overlooked the Great Pyramid display.

Looking down on it, Flynn noted that the recreation was finally complete: the Pyramid, the ruins in various states of destruction that surrounded it, the dioramas of sand dunes, even the capstone, beautifully restored—all were in their right places. Overhead, the full moon shined down through the glass roof, illuminating the entire display in its glow.

At the foot of the Pyramid, a group of about twenty members of the Serpent Brotherhood were gathered in a rough semi-circle. One of them was very familiar to Flynn: Professor Harris. He stood there with his hands in his pockets, his bowl cut blonde hair and wire-rimmed glasses, waiting with the others.

From the shadows near the tables where students had once assembled pictographs, Wilde appeared, striding confidently toward the gathered cultists. Flanking him, Rhodes and Lana dragged a handcuffed Nicole between them. She didn't appear to have been physically abused, but she did look madder than the proverbial wet hen.

Wilde spread his arms in greeting. "Serpent Brothers! Our dreams come true tonight!" He held up the three pieces of the Spear of Destiny, and the room erupted in cheers.

Watching from the balcony gave Flynn and Judson a pretty good view of the proceedings. Staring down at Wilde, Flynn said, "Doesn't that guy ever die?" He pointed. "See that fellow there? His name is Professor Harris. I should've known he was evil. He gave me an A-minus."

Judson was watching Nicole with interest. "It doesn't look like she's been doing much—what did you call it?—'cahooting.'"

Flynn smiled. "I should never have doubted her." He slowly inched back from the edge of the balcony. "Come on."

He led Judson off the balcony, toward the stairs that would take them down to the main floor. "We've got to hurry," he said. "The moon will reach its zenith any minute."

Nicole had thought she hated Edward when she first found out that he'd staged his own death and joined the Serpent Brotherhood. Hate didn't even begin to describe what she was feeling now.

He must have felt it, too, because even though he'd kept a close guard on her every second, he still glanced at her over his shoulder with something not unlike fear in his eyes. He knew that she'd kill him, given even half a chance...

After making love to Flynn, she'd fallen into a deep and restful sleep—her first in days. Late in the night, she'd half-woken when she thought she'd heard a sound, and opened her eyes in time to see a cloth coming at her face. Her struggles were short and ineffective; she was unconscious in seconds.

When she'd woken later, she was propped in an airplane seat. A silk robe had been wrapped around her to cover her nakedness, but other than that, there was no clue as to what precisely had happened.

Edward was sitting in a leather seat across from her. "Lana said you'd be waking up about now," he said. "I thought we should have a talk."

Shaking her head, still groggy, she said, "A talk?"

"Yes," he said. "About what I did to your so-called *Librarian,* and how I now have all three pieces of the Spear."

She'd lunged at him then, but that was when she discovered that she'd been tied to her seat.

"What did you do to him, Edward?" she hissed.

He'd leaned back in his seat, smiled, and said, "I gave him to Rhodes to play with for awhile."

"Rhodes!"

"Rhodes was really irritated with Flynn. He may have skinned him alive."

"You bastard," she said.

"But in any case, he *is* dead," Edward continued, as though he hadn't heard her. "And you are not. You can still join me, Nicole. Someone as talented as you shouldn't be wasted."

"Screw you," she said, feeling her heart break. "I'll die first."

Edward had stood then and slapped her once—hard—across the cheek. "You certainly will," he snapped.

Now, she watched as he lifted the Spear pieces again and said, "We call down the power of the Gods, the Ancient Ones…"

A shaft of moonlight shot through the glass ceiling and into the capstone of the Pyramid. Wilde nodded sharply to Lana and Rhodes, then turned and walked into the Pyramid.

The two thugs yanked on Nicole's handcuffs, and she stumbled forward and followed them into the recreation. After a short passage, they came to a room that literally glowed with light—the moonbeam from above came down into the direct center of the chamber.

Edward tossed the Spear pieces into the light, and as they passed through it, Nicole saw them fuse together, rising into the flow of energy. A flash of power came from the Spear as bizarre currents washed over it.

"This House, a gateway between life and death…" Edward continued, watching with rapt attention as the Spear floated and fused in the energy. "…this weapon, bathed in the blood of One who Defied Death itself…" He reached out toward the Spear. "I claim power over life and death!"

He grasped the Spear and a surge of energy blasted out. He convulsed as it surged up and down in the column of moonlight.

"I can't do this alone," Flynn whispered. He and Judson had reached an entrance archway to discover that it was guarded. "It's not really my kind of thing."

"You have me," Judson replied.

"No offense," Flynn said, "but you're—"

Judson silently reached forward and bounced the thug's head off the stone archway, then lowered him to the floor.

"—a baaad mother," Flynn finished.

"I was once a Librarian, too," Judson said. "Gave it up to take an administrative post."

"Well, that's helpful to know," Flynn said. "Anything else you'd like to share?"

Judson grinned. "Nothing comes to mind right this second."

Edward stepped out of the column of energy, grasping the restored Spear of Destiny in both hands. Power radiated from his very pores. The energy surged off him and caused his eyes to glow with a pulsing light.

This can't be good, Nicole thought.

Edward slammed the butt of the spear down on the floor with a resounding CRACK! The flagstones cobwebbed under the force of the blow.

Lana and Rhodes took a step back, and Nicole willingly followed.

Edward's face was a picture of ecstasy. "Oh, yes!" he cried. "I feel it. I feel the power. The power of life—"

He took one long stride forward—and drove the Spear into Rhodes' belly.

Rhodes looked down and grasped the Spear protruding from his abdomen. He shivered, and his face went ashen. Then he screamed—a long, drawn out cry of agony.

To Nicole, it sounded like his voice was drifting away, and that's when she realized that Rhodes' soul was literally being sucked from his body. She watched as his life force traveled the length of the Spear shaft and *into* Edward Wilde.

Edward threw his head back, taking it in. The expression on his face was almost sexual, and Nicole shuddered.

"—and the *power of death!*" he said. He spun around and tossed Rhodes' soulless husk back into the column of light. One final scream sounded from the man as his body disintegrated.

The sight of what Edward had become sent a shockwave through her body. He was completely absorbed by the power... and utterly evil.

He stepped forward, spinning the Spear with grotesque ease. "And now for you," he said.

He thrust out with the Spear—just as she felt someone slam into her, knocking her out of the way.

It was Flynn!

"Time to go now," he said. He picked her up and dragged her from the Pyramid.

Nicole allowed herself a moment of heart-surging triumph. *He's alive! He's alive! He's alive!*

Flynn fought against the rising current of panic in his chest. Wilde had changed, become something almost superhuman and very deadly. Once they reached the outside of the Pyramid, he stopped and turned to Nicole, who held her hands up. She was still in handcuffs.

He reached out and grabbed her wrists, causing the cuffs to fall to the floor. "How'd you…" she started to ask.

Flynn shrugged. "Houdini, 1926, Prague…"

Behind them, Wilde came out of the Pyramid, still bearing the Spear. The Serpent Brotherhood thugs started forward.

"Kill them!" Wilde shrieked. "Kill them *all!*"

As the cultists surged toward them, Judson scrambled over to where Flynn and Nicole stood in back-to-back fighting stances. "The Spear must be returned to the Library," he said.

Just then three of the thugs surged toward Judson. He barely blinked—just stepped calmly to one side, and grabbed two of them by the back of their necks. His quick pinching movement dropped them like rag dolls.

"Wow," Nicole said. "Impressive."

"You have to get the Spear from Wilde before he becomes too powerful," Judson said to Flynn.

"He's going to get more powerful?" Flynn asked.

"This is only the beginning of what the Spear will do to him," he said.

"Perfect," Flynn said, then turned to where Wilde had been standing in the Pyramid doorway. He watched as the Serpent Brotherhood surrounded his enemies, shrugged, and headed back into the Pyramid.

The first wave of cultists surged forward, but Judson and Nicole quickly dispatched them with a series of quick kicks and punches, opening a path for Flynn.

"Go!" Judson said.

Flynn ran for it, hoping that Nicole and Judson would be able to hold off the others. Just as he reached the entrance, Professor Harris stepped in front of him.

"I can't let you do—" he began.

Flynn punched him, straight-arm, in the nose.

Harris' hands flew up to his face, a strangled sound of pain coming from him. He held out his blood-covered hands. "You doke by dose," he said.

"Did what you said," Flynn told him. "Learned a few things out in the world."

"But you doke my dose!"

"Oh, get out of my way," Flynn muttered, and shoved him aside—which turned out to be unnecessary, since Harris took one more look at the blood and promptly fainted.

Nicole and Judson fought back-to-back. She moved with spins and kicks, while Judson barely even broke a sweat. He moved with an odd kind of grace that she appreciated. He was very good, but she sure wouldn't have guessed it to look at him.

So far, they'd been able to hold the press of cultists back, giving Flynn the time he would need to deal with Edward.

She turned to see if Flynn had gotten inside the Pyramid, and noted that Lana was closing in on him. Where had *she* come from?

"Hold them off!" she said to Judson. She turned and wheel-kicked one thug in the head, then raced off to protect her geeky charge.

She saw Lana point the gun at Flynn, heard her say, "It doesn't have to be like this! We're going to rule the world! We could be together!" The desperate sound of wanting in her voice set Nicole's teeth on edge.

And she was hitting on Flynn!

Springing forward, she slammed a fist into Lana's cheek. "Get your own geek!"

Down, but by no means out, Lana staggered back. She looked Nicole up and down and nodded, then put away her gun.

"This should be interesting," she said, going into a fighting stance. "Kicking your ass is going to be a real pleasure."

Nicole saw Flynn run into the Pyramid, then turned her attention to Lana.

"Talk all you want," she said, readying herself. She suddenly realized she was strangely pleased to be confronting this particular opponent. The little hussy. "Maybe it'll take your mind away from the pain."

They lunged at each other, screeching like banshees.

CHAPTER THIRTEEN

Wilde was standing next to the column of light, drawing even more power and energy from it.

"That's enough, Wilde," Flynn called. "Drop the Spear." It was pure bravado, especially since he didn't even have a weapon, but it seemed worth a shot.

Wilde didn't even turn around. "You're too late, Flynn. The power of the Spear is mine!"

In a blur, he spun, backhanding Flynn into the wall. The force was great enough to nearly knock him unconscious. He felt himself begin to slide down, heading for darkness.

"You're the best they could come up with to replace me?" Wilde said with a sneer. "How pathetic!"

He lunged forward, and somehow Flynn managed to roll way. The Spear shattered the stones of the wall where he'd been leaning. Wilde stabbed forward again, and missed as Flynn scrambled backward. The stone floor was vaporized into tiny fragments.

I could be in a little trouble here, Flynn thought as Wilde lunged toward him again. *Or a lot of trouble.*

"Run as much as you want, *Librarian,*" Wilde said, thrusting at him with the Spear. "But tonight you die!"

Nicole ducked as Lana threw another flurry of kicks and punches. The woman was *good,* there was little doubt about that.

She stepped back, and threw a quick elbow smash at Lana's face.

Lana blocked and returned with a stunning roundhouse that Nicole just barely managed to block.

Pressing her advantage, Lana moved in again, her fists and feet literally blurs. Nicole had all she could do to block most of them.

She caught a glimpse of the amazing Judson, who had whittled his enemies down to five. They were circling him warily, and when two of them rushed him, he executed a seemingly simple series of twists, avoiding their blows with ease. They just couldn't hit him, and judging from the smile on his face, Judson was enjoying the game.

Her momentary distraction was enough to allow Lana to connect with a quick jab and uppercut to her jaw, and Nicole reeled back.

Lana didn't even appear tired yet.

I could be in a little trouble here, she thought, moving to block another flurry of punches and kicks.

Wilde slashed out with the Spear again, and Flynn *felt* it pass, leaving his shirt in tatters. He stumbled back as his opponent moved in again. It was fortunate that Wilde wasn't an extraordinarily apt master of spear fighting, and that Flynn had recently picked up a lot of expertise on running for his life—so far, that's all that had kept him alive.

Wilde surged forward again, and Flynn leapt out of the way. The Spear connected with the wall, and stone fragments flew in a shower. He scrambled out of the way once more, tripping and stumbling as he went.

He tripped again, scraped his knees, tried to keep going, and fell to the ground. Wilde stabbed at him as he fell and missed again.

"You're too clumsy to even die properly!" he yelled, furious.

So far, the beating had been severe, as Flynn had tripped, fallen, rolled, and generally abused himself against all the stones. And Wilde was becoming more enraged and unstable with each passing second. Now he was randomly smashing at the stones of the Pyramid, whirling the Spera about his head and around his body, like a cheap Conan the Barbarian knockoff.

Flynn winced as rock fragments stung his face. His body felt battered and bruised from head to toe. "You say that now," he called, "but I did quite a bit more than dance with your girl—"

Wilde spun and Flynn felt the Spear hit him, driving him back into the wall with a resounding *thunk!* He gasped, the breath leaving his body, and looked down, expecting the worst.

It was the wrong end of the spear! Wilde had caught him with the butt-end, rather than the point, as he'd spun it.

Now he stepped back, twirled it again, prepared to impale Flynn like a piece of fruit. Flynn waited, then jumped out of the way, rolling, as the Spear missed him and pierced the stone of the Pyramid, shattering it.

Wilde screamed in frustration and turned to come after him once more.

Lucky, Flynn thought, trying to keep moving. *But he won't make that mistake again.*

Nicole's face was bruised, and she knew that if she didn't do something to end this quickly, Lana would finish her. The woman was a master martial-artist, and try as she might, Nicole couldn't stop all of her kicks and punches.

Another flurry came at her and several more stung her cheeks, driving her backward and making her eyes water.

Lana paused, grinning. "Don't worry, darling. You can die assured that the Librarian will be in far more capable hands than yours." She held out her own. "He'll be in mine!"

There were basically two schools of thought on hand-to-hand combat. The first suggested that one principally use defensive techniques until an opening presented itself. The second theorized that it was better to attack than defend. Nicole herself, furious, invented a third school of thought on the spot: kill the bitch and be done with it.

She charged forward. Flynn would *not* belong to this woman! She began spinning, leaping into the air in a series of wheel kicks that drove Lana back, stunned by the savage turn of Nicole's attack.

"Keep your grubby hands to yourself!" Nicole screamed. She landed a roundhouse kick to Lana's temple, and the woman crumbled to the floor, unconscious.

"I love him," Nicole said quietly, staring at her fallen opponent.

The stones of the Pyramid were shattering with rapid-fire speed as Wilde spun and thrust with the Spear. Flynn was doing his best to dodge both the Spear and the flying pieces of stone, but was tired. His body ached, and he had innumerable cuts and bruises. He was dizzy and having a harder and harder time keeping away from Wilde.

Finally, he stumbled one time too many. Wilde reached out and snatched him by the ragged remains of his shirt. He lifted him off his feet, one-handed.

"Time's up," Wilde said.

Dazed, Flynn said, "Bite me, Serpent Boy."

Wilde looked at the center of the Pyramid where the pillar of light and energy was glowing still—an intense ray of pure power and energy.

"Goodbye, Librarian," Wilde said—and threw Flynn across the room.

There was a brief flash of light as he crossed into the beam, a flicker of... something. Then he landed on the floor and the light was gone.

The interior of the Pyramid was suddenly dark, almost silent.

"What?" Flynn heard Wilde say.

Somehow, Flynn managed to get to his feet. He looked around in satisfaction. The floor was littered with the shattered fragments of the stone walls and floor. Breathing hard, he said, "If any of the support stones... are off by even... an inch..."

"What?" Wilde said again, uncomprehending.

"...the Pyramid collapses," Flynn finished.

A low, thrumming groan sounded in the walls around them. Wilde turned in circles, the beginnings of panic in his eyes. Flynn picked up a hunk of stone from the floor.

"I'd say *this* was out of alignment." The stone crumbled to dust in his fist.

"You're nothing!" Wilde said. "I will destroy you."

Flynn shook his head. "You never will. You know why? Because the things that make life worth living do not come from here—"

Wilde charged, roaring, and Flynn ducked, connecting with a brutal punch to Wilde's head. He staggered.

"—they come from here!" Flynn yelled. He palm-punched forward, slamming his hands into Wilde's chest.

Wilde stumbled backward, tumbling into the center of the room where the pillar of light had been.

The roar in the walls grew louder and louder, becoming a freight train of sound. Wilde covered his ears, his shocked expression a mix of pain and outrage. Stones began to rain down from above.

Flynn stepped back, knowing what was about to happen. He pointed up, and Wilde looked in time to see the capstone falling toward him—an unstoppable block of stone weighing tons.

"Look out," Flynn whispered, then smiled. "Oh, too late."

Wilde's eyes went wide just before the capstone crushed him like a bug. The impact knocked the Spear out of his hands and it went flying upward, spinning end-over-end...

Flynn stretched out his hand and caught it in one smooth motion.

"That should just about do it," he said, then turned and made for the exit.

Debris and smoke rolled out of the entrance to the Great Pyramid, and the roaring sound of its collapse filled the museum. Nicole checked the knots on Lana's bonds once more, and rushed to where Judson was staring down his last two attackers. She took up a position next to him.

"Leave now," Judson said to them, "while you can still speak in a lower register."

The thugs took one look at the unconscious bodies of their comrades littering the floor—most of them put there by this opponent—then turned and ran out of the building.

Judson laughed, then pointed toward the Pyramid.

As the building collapsed, Flynn staggered out of the dust cloud—clutching the Spear of Destiny in his hands.

He looks absolutely terrible, Nicole thought, seeing his ragged shirt and the scratches and bruises covering his body. *And absolutely wonderful, too.*

Flynn nodded to her as he reached them, then tossed the Spear to Judson. "I believe," he said, "that this belongs in the Library."

Judson beamed with pride. "I believe you're right," he said.

Nicole smiled at Flynn, then took him in her arms. "I thought you were dead," she said, kissing him.

"You seem to have that problem with the men in your life," Flynn said.

"Do not!" she protested. "Just two."

Flynn chuckled and kissed her again. "Well," he said, glancing back at the ruined Pyramid. "You've only got one to worry about now."

"Come on, kids," Judson said. "Let's call it a night."

They left the museum together, walking arm in arm. Behind them, Judson whistled a happy tune. Once again, the right Librarian had been chosen.

Tomorrow, he'd prove it to Flynn.

Flynn watched as Judson carefully placed the fully restored Spear of Destiny in its case. Charlene polished the glass.

"Someday," she was saying, "we'll have to figure out how to sever the Spear and once again hide the pieces."

"Sounds like a job for some *future* Librarian," Flynn quipped. "You know, maybe one who's not on his probationary period and who's been assigned a parking space."

He wasn't too banged up, though Nicole had insisted on a very *thorough* examination the night before, and had bandaged several of his more serious wounds. He glanced around the collection again, seeing what it truly represented to the future of mankind.

Nearby, the legendary sword Excalibur was still lodged in its stone. He remembered what Judson had said. "… only the worthy…"

Wondering, Flynn reached out for the hilt. He hesitated, then grasped it firmly. It pulled from the stone with ease.

There was no triumphant surge of feeling in this moment, no giddiness, and Flynn considered two possibilities: that he couldn't have pulled the sword from the stone until he'd done all the tasks associated with recovering the Spear… or that he could have done it all along.

He stared at Excalibur, considering carefully what this might mean, but then he heard Judson and Charlene calling for him.

Flynn put the sword back in the stone and walked to where they stood at the wall of history—the one with all the portraits of previous Librarians. Edward Wilde's was conspicuously absent. Charlene was primping at a curtain.

"We thought you'd like to see this, Flynn," Judson said. He nodded at Charlene, who pulled a cord, dropping the curtain to the floor.

Behind it was a painting of Flynn, holding the Spear of Destiny in a triumphant pose.

"You *are* worthy," Judson said. "You've proven that already."

"Probationary period is over," Charlene said. "But don't think I won't dock your pay if you're late or if you break anything." She smiled. "I *will*."

Flynn smiled. "Thank you," he said simply.

Then he turned and walked back into the collection—the Library of Sciences Unknown—and he knew that he was home.

EPILOGUE

Three Months Later

The sidewalk café wasn't overly crowded, but Flynn's mom had no trouble at all spotting three young women at a nearby table to harangue. And embarrass the daylights out of him.

"Flynn may be a librarian now," she was telling them, "but he's capable of so much more if he just had the right woman to push him."

"Mom…" Flynn said.

"Like you," Margie said, pointing to one. "Or you," she added, pointing to another.

"Mom…" he tried again.

"Not you," Margie said, pointing to the last of the three. "You'd eat him alive. I can tell."

Exasperated, Flynn raised his voice. "Mom!"

She turned her attention back to him. "What is it, dear?"

"You don't understand," he said. "Being a Librarian is actually a pretty cool job. I get to do some great things."

"Yeah, like what?" she said, obviously trying to humor him.

Flynn remembered the first time he'd been in the Library, chasing the jetpack past a blasé Judson. "I get to *serve* the public by maintaining accurate records of Library holdings," he said.

"Sounds exciting," she said.

He thought back to when Nicole literally threw him out of the airplane without a parachute. "I *safeguard* the staff in the proper use of Library materials," he added.

"Safety's practically your middle name, dear," Margie said. "I'm sure they feel very safe around you."

He remembered the terrifying take-off of the helicopter, his desperate attempt to pilot the thing. "*And,*" he said, "*sacrifice* everything for an effective Library."

Margie and the young women stared at him, their expressions blank. Flynn waved a hand in front of them. "Hello?" he said. "Come on, it's not that boring!"

"I'm sorry, dear," Margie said. "What were you saying?"

"Mom, stop that!"

She laughed. "I'm just trying to help you is all," she said. "A mother wants her son to find love, you know."

"And I've told you that you don't have to fix me up anymore, right?"

"Oh, yes," Margie said. "The ever-mysterious Nicole. She's never quite around to meet your mother, is she?"

"It's… complicated," Flynn said. "I've tried to explain that."

Before his mother could answer, the sound of screeching brakes and a roaring engine echoed in the street. Flynn turned in time to see a motorcycle fly through the air, going over the hedge bordering the café; it landed hard between the dining tables. The driver, dressed in a full suit of black leather with a visored helmet, slammed on the brakes again and spun the bike in a circle, bringing it to a stop next to Flynn's table.

Everyone was dead silent, but Flynn's experiences as The Librarian had inured him from easy panic. He arched an eyebrow as the rider pulled off her helmet, and shook out a beautiful mane of hair.

"Hey, studmuffin," Nicole said.

Flynn grinned. "Nicole, meet my mom," he said. Seeing his mother's stunned expression, he added, "Mom, meet Nicole. My girlfriend."

"Nice to meet you finally, Mrs. Carson," Nicole said.

Coming around a bit, Margie managed a hesitant, "The... the pleasure is mine."

Nicole turned her attention back to Flynn. "The Deadly Scorpion League found H.G. Wells' Time Machine," she said. "We have to go and get it from them."

"The 'Deadly Scorpion League'?" Flynn asked. "What is it with bad guys and bizarre animal and insect names for their cults?"

Nicole shrugged. "Eh," she said. "Who knows?"

Flynn stood up and started to get on the back of the motorcycle—when he noticed that Nicole was smiling. His expression fell.

"Oh, no," he said. "You're smiling. Why are you smiling?"

"Because there's about a dozen time-traveling ninjas waiting to kill us," she said. She kissed the tip of his nose.

Flynn sighed heavily, sat down on the saddle, and wrapped his arms around her waist.

"Psychopath," he said.

"Geek," she replied. Then she kick-started the bike.

"Bye, Mom!" Flynn said. "I'll call you!"

"Nice meeting you, Mrs. Carson," Nicole said, then gunned the engine.

She jumped it into the street, just as a swarm of vehicles rounded the corner.

"Oh, good," she said. "Here they come now!"

"Perfect," Flynn said. "Just perfect."

Nicole guided the bike around a sharp corner, and they were gone.

ABOUT THE AUTHOR

CHRISTOPHER TRACY lives with his family and a varied number of animals, both domestic and wild, on a secluded ranch not all that far from Tombstone, Arizona. In addition to writing film and television novelizations, he also pens the occasional bit of mediocre poetry.

When he's not busy writing or tracking through the desert, Christopher works with horses, plays the guitar, and raises German Shepherd-Wolf hybrids, two of which patrol his property for unwelcome guests and intruders.